'You're ver...

D0756711

Dear Reader,

I came out of a horrid five-year relationship once, feeling hurt, dejected and jaded. It hadn't been a good place to be—mentally or emotionally—and I emerged from the experience as a single woman, utterly determined never to get involved in another relationship ever again. Men were off the menu.

Three weeks later I was engaged to be married to my now husband! No one—definitely not me!—could have predicted that I would be swept so swiftly off my feet and find a wonderful, kind, loving man who could disprove all my theories about men in one fell swoop.

It's a shock to the system, I can tell you, and I wanted to write about and explore that shock—and that's how my characters in this book, Naomi and Tom, came into being. They both have preconceived ideas about love and I wanted to shake their worlds!

I felt every second of Naomi's journey, and I wrote about a hero whom I hope all of my readers can fall in love with. I certainly did! I hope you'll enjoy their story.

Louisa xxx

ONE
LIFE-CHANGING
NIGHT

BY
LOUISA HEATON

MILLS & BOON

Published in Great Britain 2016
By Mills & Boon, an imprint of HarperCollins*Publishers*
1 London Bridge Street, London, SE1 9GF

© 2016 Louisa Heaton

ISBN: 978-0-263-25437-2

Our policy is to use papers that are natural, renewable and recyclable
products and made from wood grown in sustainable forests. The logging
and manufacturing processes conform to the legal environmental
regulations of the country of origin.

Printed and bound in Spain
by CPI, Barcelona

Louisa Heaton lives on Hayling Island, Hampshire, with her husband, four children and a small zoo. She has worked in various roles in the health industry—most recently four years as a Community First Responder, answering 999 calls. When not writing, Louisa enjoys other creative pursuits, including reading, quilting and patchwork—usually instead of the things she ought to be doing!

Books by Louisa Heaton

Mills & Boon Medical Romance

The Baby That Changed Her Life
His Perfect Bride?
A Father This Christmas?

Visit the Author Profile page
at millsandboon.co.uk for more titles.

For Sukidoo, the best friend I've never met. xx

CHAPTER ONE

SHE HADN'T EXPECTED to fall into the arms of a stunningly handsome man on her first day at work. Or to have climbed up a wobbly ladder in Welbeck Memorial's A&E department. But it was nearly the end of January and the Christmas decorations were *still* up.

Naomi had offered to take them down at the end of her shift, which had been a long twelve hours, and her head was buzzing with information and protocols and procedures. But she had nothing waiting for her at home—not even a cat—and, quite frankly, putting off going back to her little bedsit with its dingy second-hand furniture had seemed like a good option. Starting a new life was one thing, but starting it in a derelict, ought-to-be-bulldozed ground-floor flat with a growing mould problem was another.

When she'd offered to take the decorations down, the sister in charge had been very sweet. 'Oh, you don't have to do that! We'll get one of the porters to do it. It's your first day.'

But she'd insisted. 'Honestly, it's fine. Besides, it's bad luck to keep them up this long. Bringing the old year into the new.'

'Well, just be careful. There's a stepladder in my office you can use, but make sure you get someone to steady it for you, or you'll have Health and Safety on my back.'

Naomi smiled to herself, remembering the health and safety lecture she'd sat through that morning. She would be sensible and follow the rules. Just as she'd always done. She located the boxes for the Christmas decorations piled high in the sister's office and spent the first hour removing baubles and tinsel from the lower branches.

The old, artificial tree was almost bald in parts and she could see it was decades old, dragged out from its box year after year to try and brighten the place up. Her nose wrinkled as she leant too far into one of the branches and breathed in dust and the smell of Christmases past.

As she pulled her face free of the tree, another stench—this one of alcohol and body odour—mixed into the fray, sweeping over her like a wave. A scruffy-looking man with stained clothes staggered towards her. She turned to steady him as he passed by, hoping to steer him back in the direction of the waiting room, but the drunk angrily turned on her instead. 'Leave me alone! Shouldn't you be *working* instead of playing with that tree? I've been waiting to be seen for *ages* and you're out here messing around!'

They often saw people who were drunk in Accident and Emergency and Naomi knew they were mostly unthreatening. All she had to do was be non-confrontational and pleasant and they would be satisfied.

She smiled and led him back into the waiting room. 'You'll be seen soon, sir, don't worry.'

'Bloomin' patronising me! You should be working!' he slurred.

She saw no point in telling him she'd already worked a twelve-hour shift and that she ought to have been at home by now. He didn't want to hear that. He wanted to hear that he would be treated. 'I'm sure it won't be long now.'

Once he was settled back into his chair, she went back to the tree. To get the decorations down from the top she needed to go up the ladder. And that meant she needed someone to help steady it.

She headed back into the unit, looking for someone who was free, but everyone was so busy. And she didn't know anyone well enough yet to interrupt their work and ask them to help her. Because what was more important? Patient care, or an old tree?

Naomi looked down the long corridor at the stepladder. It wasn't that high. Just three steps. What harm would it do, if she was quick? Surely Matron wouldn't like her taking away a member of staff to hold a *ladder* when they could be *treating* someone.

Hmm. I'll be careful. These health and safety measures are always too cautious anyway.

She positioned the ladder where she needed it, noticing that it was a little uneven, and gave a quick look around to make sure no one was about to pounce and tell her off, and climbed up. She picked off the first few baubles and strings of tinsel and dropped them into the cardboard boxes beneath, hearing them plop into the decorations below. She worked quickly, steadying herself when she felt the ladder wobble a bit beneath her feet. The star on the top of the tree was just a tiny bit out of her reach and so she leant for it, stretching. The ladder wobbled even more so and she felt it start to move beneath her. 'Oh!'

She felt herself fall and braced herself for the impact and the hard, unforgiving floor. But instead, her fall was broken by a solid, reassuring pair of arms.

Stunned, she looked up to say thank you, but her voice somehow got stuck in her throat.

This man was nothing like the drunk that had accosted her a moment ago. *This* man had captivating eyes of cerulean blue, a strong jawline and he smelt just…heavenly! Masculine and invigorating.

'Whoa! Are you mad?' *That voice.* The most perfect accent she'd ever heard. Refined. Educated. Even if it was currently scolding her.

She blushed madly as she stared up into his eyes, her breath catching in her throat. She was embarrassed at having fallen. Ashamed at having been caught up the ladder when she'd been *told* to get someone to help her and desperately doing her level best to appear normal and not swoon like a heroine in a romance novel. She'd been determined to move to London and start life as a strong, confident, independent woman and yet here she was: it was only her first day at work and she was lying in a man's arms.

A very handsome man's arms! Her cheeks flamed with heat as he easily stood her upright, making sure she was steady before he let her go. When he did, she almost felt disappointed to be out of those arms, but…*oh!*

He was tall, almost a head taller than her, well past six foot, and he had the most startling blue eyes she'd ever seen. He was looking her over, assessing her, his gaze questioning.

She managed to find some words. 'Thank you, I… shouldn't have been up there.' She blushed again, brushing her hands down her clothes as if she were covered in dust and dirt. She wasn't. She just didn't know what else to do and she had to do *something*! Naomi had never been held in a man's arms like that. Cradled. Protected. Vincent had never held her that way. Not that that was his fault.

This man was probably used to women blushing in front of him. Women fawning at his feet, unable to string a sentence together.

He was dressed smartly in what had to be a tailored bespoke suit that fitted his finely toned body to perfection. This man knew how to dress and he dressed well, his clothes accentuating his best features. A red scarf slung casually around his neck highlighted the auburn tones in his hair.

Still, she wasn't going to let herself be blown away by a gorgeous man. She knew men like this usually came with health warnings.

Get involved at your own risk.

Look at what had happened to her mother, for instance.

She wasn't even sure who he was. She looked for the badge that all hospital employees wore, but couldn't see it.

'You must be new here?' She saw him glance at *her* name badge.

'Naomi.' She reached out her hand to shake his. 'Bloom. A&E nurse. First day.'

He looked at her hand briefly as if she were offering him a handful of sputum. Then he ignored it. 'Tom Williams. Clinical Lead and doctor. Almost *your* doctor for that stunt you just pulled.'

She faltered, her hand dropping away from him. This was her boss? She looked away, trying to think quickly, before returning her gaze to his. 'I'm sorry, I—'

'You had your induction this morning?' If this had been any other situation, she could have listened to his voice all day. It was rich and warm, classy. It was the sort of voice you heard from an English villain in an American movie.

Focus.

'I did, but—'

He smiled at her but the smile didn't reach his eyes. 'The health and safety briefing was covered?'

She nodded, feeling like a naughty child who was standing in front of a headmaster. 'Yes, but I didn't want to pull anyone away from their work, as they were all so busy, so I thought I'd do it myself.' The words burbled out of her quickly, showing her horror at having been caught so badly in the wrong.

She'd assumed she had been doing the right thing. Naomi had learnt the value of being able to do something for yourself. It was a pleasure denied to many people. A normality that they craved. To be able to do simple things like opening their own cupboard to reach for a mug, or taking themselves to the toilet. On their own. Without someone to help them.

He glanced at the tree. 'Well, luckily I managed to save you from a sprained ankle. Or something worse.' He shrugged his shoulders. 'A sprained neck wouldn't have gone down well on your first day. Nor would me having to fill in a three-page incident-report form after I've just spent twenty hours on non-stop duty.'

'I'm sorry, Dr Williams.'

Tom frowned, seeming concerned as he looked around them and over towards the waiting area. 'Who asked you to do this?'

She shrugged. 'I volunteered.'

'You volunteered?' He let out a short, impatient sigh. 'Well, if you're going to insist on doing this, I'd better stay and make sure you're safe.'

'Oh, you don't have to—'

'You might head back up that ladder. Besides, I was only on my way home.' He placed his folded coat down on top of his briefcase, removed his scarf and rolled up his sleeves.

He had beautiful forearms... Smooth. Strong.

If he hadn't just given her a dressing-down, she might have been tempted to appreciate them a bit more. 'Right. Erm…thanks.'

He looked the tree up and down. 'This old tree ought to have been passed through a chipper years ago.'

'I don't think they do that to fake trees.'

'No. Probably not.'

He started to take off some more of the decorations that he could reach just by standing there, which Naomi hadn't had a chance in hell of reaching, and then he passed them to her, so she could put them in their boxes a little more carefully than she'd been doing earlier. She hated feeling like a chastised child and wanted to get back on a more even keel, so she ventured some basic conversation. 'So you've worked here for a while, then?'

He glanced at her. 'Yes. What made you come to Welbeck?'

He didn't need to know her history. He probably didn't even want to know. He was just being polite. Or, at least, as polite as he could be.

She'd already vowed not to mention her past to anyone here. She didn't want pity or sympathy. She just wanted to get on with her life. If she told people she'd come out of a marriage where she'd been more of a carer than a wife, they tended to look at her with pity.

'I used to live in the East Midlands, originally, but I fancied a change of pace, so I got myself a cheap bedsit down here and hoped for the best.' This was better conversation, she thought. Much better than being told off.

'I thought I heard an accent.'

She smiled, never having thought of herself as someone with an accent. 'Really?'

'Yes. Bit of a northern twang. I'll go up the ladder and get the rest of them.'

'Be my guest.' She held it steady as he went up and together they made a quick, efficient team. The tree was soon naked of ornaments, broken down into its segments and boxed away for next year. Naomi quickly swept up the debris. It hadn't taken them more than fifteen minutes to get it sorted. 'Thanks for the help. It was really kind of you.'

'No problem.' He seemed to look at her for a moment longer than was comfortable, then suddenly shook his head at whatever thought he'd had and picked up his coat and briefcase. 'Let's try not to get hurt tomorrow, Nurse Bloom, hmm?'

'Course not.' She watched him walk away and let out a breath that she hadn't been aware she'd been holding.

Wow. What a bear!

And he was her boss! That was embarrassing. Her first day and she had already been caught breaking a rule, although thankfully not breaking anything else.

She determined to try and stay out of Dr Williams's way as much as possible. She would only let him notice her when she was being brilliant, providing outstanding nursing care.

She headed in the other direction and went to fetch her coat.

The weather was doing its best to let the people of London know that it was winter. There'd been snow a few days ago and, though there'd been nothing since, it was still on the ground, due to the freezing temperatures. The surrounding buildings looked grey, damp and cold and as Naomi came out of the hospital to head for home—a place she really didn't want to go, knowing it would be just as awful inside as it was out—she wrapped her knitted green scarf around her tightly and pulled on her gloves.

There were people standing outside the entrance to A&E puffing away on cigarettes, their hands cupped around them, as if somehow gaining a small measure of warmth. One of them was the drunk that had confronted Naomi earlier and he looked up, catching her gaze with vehemence. He came staggering back over to her, the overwhelming stench of body odour and stale alcohol almost overpowering. With one grimy finger he pushed her in the chest. '*You* lot kept me waiting.'

Naomi felt disconcerted. And a little afraid. She could handle this sort of aggression when she was at work. In the hospital. Then she had her uniform on and was surrounded by people who she knew would come to her aid. Violence against hospital staff wasn't tolerated and they had security guards, too. But out here, outside work, in her normal clothes, she felt more vulnerable.

'Look, sir—'

'You lot…kept me *waiting*!' He gave her another shove and she stumbled backwards, caught off balance, her heart pounding. What a first day she was having. She'd wound up her new boss and now she was being accosted by a member of the public. She held up her hands as if in surrender and backed away, afraid of what might happen, when suddenly a tall figure stepped between them.

It was Tom. He had stepped in, towering over the drunk like a menacing gladiator.

'Step away.' He dropped his briefcase to the floor without taking his eyes off the belligerent man and then slowly walked towards him.

Naomi watched, open-mouthed in shock. It had to be him! Rescuing her again!

What must he think of me?

'What *you* gonna do? Huh? I know my rights!' A small piece of spittle flew from the man's mouth, but his swagger and bravado soon dissipated as Tom continued to step towards him.

'If you *ever* touch a member of my staff again, you'll find yourself in a police cell quicker than you could ever imagine.'

The man staggered backwards, blinking. 'All right! All right! I'm going!' He looked most put out that his bullying tactics hadn't worked and he'd been knocked back by a better, stronger man. 'You lot are all the same!' He shuffled off, muttering, his cigarette smoke surrounding him like a dirty cloud.

Tom watched him go, his coat collar turned up around his neck. Only when he was convinced that the drunk was far enough away did he turn around to look at Naomi, his gaze checking her for any injury, concern in his eyes. 'Are you all right?' His voice held a note of the same concern.

She nodded quickly. Briefly. She was unable to believe how quickly the situation had escalated.

'Mick's a frequent flyer here. Often presents drunk. He's lonely, I think.' His voice had an odd tone, but whatever he'd been thinking disappeared from his face when he turned again to make sure Mick had truly gone.

'But still he has a go at the people trying to help him.'

He smiled, disarming her. 'It happens.'

'You can say that again.' She watched Mick from afar, glad that Tom had intervened. Although she felt she would have handled it, if she'd had to. She'd taken kick-boxing classes once, years ago. She had needed something intensely physical to do, seeing as it wasn't required in her marriage. At home, she'd had to be careful in everything she did, walking on eggshells, making sure she made no dramatic movements so as not to cause inadvertent injury. Being extra careful all of the time had just seemed to emphasise her natural clumsiness. By the end, her marriage had been a physical prison.

'Thanks again. It seems you've rescued me twice in one day.' She tried to break the tension she was feeling by making a joke. 'You really ought to be wearing shining armour and riding a white horse, or something.'

He just stared at her, his face impassive.

Not a lover of jokes either. Okay.

'Anyway. Thank you.'

'Will you get home all right?'

She nodded and pulled up the collar of her own coat. 'It's not far. Just around the corner, to be honest. St Bartholomew's Road.'

'Then I'll walk you home. Mick could still be a bother. I know him and he doesn't always do what's wise.'

She couldn't let him do that. He'd done enough for her today and, besides, she didn't need him witnessing the dump she was living in. That would be too embarrassing. By his expensive clothes, she could tell this was a man that probably lived in a penthouse apartment. He'd take one look at her bedsit and then what would he think of her? He probably already thought of her as incompetent and she didn't want him thinking of her as some sort of Cinderella figure.

'You don't have to.'

'I do.' He smiled. 'You've almost fallen once today. If you fell on the ice now, it would undo all of my previous hard work.'

Naomi smiled back, her grin almost freezing into place in the bitter wind.

Right. I just won't invite him in. Then he won't understand how bad it is. I can do this. He's not a complete ogre.

'Okay.'

They walked along at a pleasant pace. There was a large park by the hospital and, this late in the day, it was filled with people walking their dogs, or couples strolling hand in hand. Naomi always noticed people doing that. It had been something denied to her and Vincent. She'd always been pushing his wheelchair.

But today, instead, she caught herself sneaking looks at
Tom and even though she tried to stop herself—sure that
he would notice—she kept doing it.

He was so good-looking; tall and broad, yet slim. He
frightened her. Not just because he was her boss and probably thought she was an incompetent nincompoop, but because he was without a doubt the most handsome man she
had ever met. Handsome men, in her experience, caused
trouble. They had certainly caused enough for her mother,
who had brought back endless strings of attractive men.
Fast-car driving, exquisitely clothed, silver-tongued indi-
viduals, so slick you'd have trouble distinguishing them
from a vat of oil. Each man had caused their own problems.
Borrowing money, never calling, one even taking his hand
to her mother. Each and every one had been heartache and
pain in a well-dressed suit. Each of them had broken her
mother's easily led heart.

That was why Naomi had fallen so easily in love with
Vincent. Why she had married him. He'd been none of
those things. He'd been average-looking, physically disabled. She'd always known where she was with him. She'd
always known the expectations. It had been simple. And
there'd been no worry or risk of him running off, having
an affair and breaking her heart.

'So how was your first day at Welbeck? *Scintillating*
health and safety briefing aside?'

Naomi looked back at the road, busy with cars. 'It was
good. Exhausting, but good. I'll be glad to get a decent
night's sleep. You? Did you have a busy day?'

*See? I can do this. Pretend this is normal. There's noth-
ing more to it than one colleague walking another home,
to ensure her safety. Having a normal conversation.*

'Yes.'

'Why did you choose A&E as a discipline?'

'It's busy.'

She waited, assuming that he'd say more, but when he didn't, she didn't push him. They were both still strangers to each other. Perhaps he had personal reasons for his career that he didn't feel like sharing with someone he'd only just met. After all, she was keeping secrets, too. Holding things back. He was entitled to do the same.

Naomi adjusted her scarf. 'You know, it's not far now. You're probably coming out of your way to walk me home, so you can go, if you want to. I don't think I'm going to get mugged in the next fifty metres.'

He turned to her. 'You don't like people helping you, do you?'

She blew out a breath. 'I stand on my own two feet. I've got used to looking after myself and I like it. The independence. The freedom.' She couldn't tell him how much that meant to her. Being out in the world and doing her own thing without having to think of anyone else. She hadn't been able to do that for a very long time.

They continued to walk, turning into her road, and she felt twisting snakes of nervousness swirl around in her stomach the closer they got.

She knew what he would think. He would see the small front yard, littered with an old settee and someone's old fridge. The detritus and litter from what seemed like a million previous tenants—empty glass milk bottles, old cans, raggedy bits of clothing, dirtied by the weather and constant stream of car exhaust fumes. And if he got past her front door? Well, she'd tried her best to pretty the place up. She had done what she could, but it never seemed enough. The truth was, she couldn't afford anywhere better and it would have to do until she'd gathered some more savings for a small deposit elsewhere.

Naomi estimated she had another six months of being

here, before she could try and rent somewhere else. 'I hope you don't think I'm rude.'

He laughed to himself. 'I can cope with rude.'

'Well, I don't mean to be.' As they came to a halt outside her front garden she hesitated, sucking in a breath, her back turned to the property. 'Well, this is me. Unfortunately.'

Tom smiled and looked past her. The smile dropped from his glorious face in an instant. 'Did you leave your front door open?'

'Er…no. Why?' Naomi turned around and instantly saw the splintering down the door frame where someone had pried it open. She gasped and went to take a step forward, but Tom gripped her arm, holding her back.

'Stay here. Call the police.'

'You're not *going in*?' Whoever had broken in could still be in there! He had no idea what he would be walking into. There was splintered wood all over the place and goodness knew what they'd done to all her things inside. He could trip on anything, hurt himself. The burglars could be waiting with weapons. It was dangerous, and…

He's not Vincent. Tom can handle himself.

He'd certainly shown himself to be capable when he'd sent Mick away outside the hospital. He'd had no hesitation about stepping into the fray there.

'Just stay here.' He laid a comforting hand upon her arm and then he was gone, darting through the doorway like an avenger, keen to surprise whoever might still be inside.

Naomi pulled her phone from her coat pocket and stabbed at the buttons, dialling for the police. Once she'd reported the break-in, she stepped towards her flat, her legs trembling, her knees weak.

She'd heard no sounds from within. No sudden clashing of Titans, no battle, no fight for survival. Whoever had broken in must be long gone. Feeling sick, she peered through the doorway. 'Dr Williams?'

'It's okay. You can come in, there's no one here!'

She stepped forward, into the small hall and then through the doorway to her lounge-kitchen.

It was as if a typhoon had swept through it. Sofa cushions had been tossed around, her coffee table knocked over and broken, her books strewn all over the floor. The few pictures she'd found at a market—nothing special, just bright prints—were on the floor, their frames smashed, the glass cracked and broken.

All of her precious belongings had been tossed around, as if they were nothing but rubbish at a dump. The sense of loss and devastation was overwhelming. With her hand over her face, she began to feel a tremble overtake her body, until she was shuddering and shaking, sobs gasping from her body as if every intake of breath were a desperate struggle for survival.

Tom frowned from his place in the kitchen and stood awkwardly as she cried.

She had no idea how long she stood there like that, just crying. For the loss of her things, for the loss of her privacy, for the uncaring way in which her things had been used and tossed aside. She'd never claimed to be rich, or to have expensive objects that she treasured, but this had been her very first venture out into the world to stand on her own two feet alone. The items she'd gathered in that home might have been from car boot sales or markets or pound shops, but they'd been *hers*. They'd each been treasured and valued as they'd arrived in her home to take their place and make the hole that she was living in a beautiful, homely place to be. Or at least, an attempt at one.

That someone had forced their way in, breaking and trashing everything…well, it broke her heart. So she cried.

And she cried. Until suddenly she realised she wasn't crying any more and Tom had started trying to sort through her belongings. He'd been picking up books and ornaments, trying to straighten them, trying to return them to their rightful place.

She couldn't look him in the eye. Had she not embarrassed herself enough in front of this man, today? Falling from a ladder. Being rescued from a drunk. Being heard as she cried like a baby? That last had been the most horrifying. It was embarrassing. Crying always made other people feel incredibly awkward and she didn't need to look at him to know how much he wanted to leave, but was staying because he now felt obligated.

What am I putting this man through, today? The impression I'm making is terrible!

'It's okay, you can go. I'll wait here for the police. I'll deal with it. You must have things to do.'

'I'll stay.'

She found an old tissue in her pocket and she pulled it out to wipe her nose and then dab at her eyes. She must look a sight! Her eyes would be all puffy and her face all red...

'No, really, you don't have to...'

'I'll stay until you're done with the police. Then, you'll need someplace to go. I won't feel safe with you sleeping here on your own tonight. It won't be secure.'

'The police will fix the door.'

'With a sheet of *plyboard*. Hardly Fort Knox. I won't leave you here with that as your sole defence against the world in this neighbourhood.'

A short brief smile found its way onto her ravaged features. She was appreciative of his kindness. He clearly wasn't all gruffness. 'Thank you.'

'Now you ought to check to see if anything's missing.'

She nodded. He was right. There were only a few things that really meant anything to her. Her photos of her and Vincent. Her old wedding ring in her bedside table that she never wore to work, as jewellery wasn't allowed.

Alone in the bedroom, she made the grim discovery that the ring was gone, stolen. Along with some cheaper bits of jewellery that she'd bought and an old watch.

She felt strangely empty as she recounted what was missing to the police when they arrived.

Throughout it all, Tom was kind and attentive. He just sat there and listened to her ramble, making them both a cup of tea and heaping hers with sugar for the shock.

Although it had been caused by a terrible situation, Naomi found herself enjoying their conversation. Just sitting and talking to someone. Something she hadn't truly experienced since Vincent had passed. She missed him greatly, but she knew he was in a better place. No longer in pain. No longer a prisoner in his own body. No longer feeling guilty for what he'd done to her life.

So it was nice just to sit and talk. Even if it was only happening because she'd been burgled!

Her first day at work had gone fine. It was only the things that had happened *after* her shift that had been so awful! Now, after being berated by her boss and saved by him from physical assault, she was being comforted by him. He might not be the most smiley individual in the world, but he was being kind.

'You need to pack some clothes for an overnight stay.'

'Right.' He was right. Being practical would also help to take her mind off what had happened. She couldn't stay here. The place felt violated. Dirty. She didn't want to have to stay there a moment longer than she had to.

'You're right...'

'What is it?'

She bit her lip. 'I have nowhere to go.'

'You must have family?'

'They're all up north. A four-hour drive away.'

He frowned. 'Friends?'

'I've just moved here. I don't know anyone.'

'Of course not.' He let out a heavy sigh, his hands on his hips. 'A hotel?'

She winced at having to admit it. 'I couldn't afford it.'

'Right. I suppose you'll have to come to mine, then. For the night. I can take you to work in the morning, too.'

Naomi tried hard not to show how horrified she was by the thought of having to share a living space with the one man whom she'd humiliated herself in front of so much today.

She couldn't stay at his. They'd only just met and, yes, he was her boss, but he was also a prickly individual, standoffish and cool. He already clearly thought of her as incompetent and now he was offering to share his home with her...

Seriously...she couldn't accept his offer.

'That's very gracious of you, but—'

'Then it's settled. Pack your things and let's get going.'

Her mouth dropped open for a moment and when she became aware that she probably looked like a landed gold-fish, she closed it again and headed to her bedroom.

I can't believe I'm doing this.

CHAPTER TWO

NAOMI WAS IN her bedroom, packing her clothes into a suitcase, as Tom sat on the torn-up sofa and stared into space.

Nurse Naomi Bloom.

What had happened?

He'd been his usual work-focused self. He'd been on call all night in the hospital and then he'd worked a full twelve-hour shift in A&E on top of that. He always did what was needed. Worked hard. He treated patients and kept his mind on work.

It was what worked for him. The work was a salve. A sticking plaster over the savage gash that was his heart. If he worked, if he took care of patients, if he investigated *their* ills, then he didn't have to focus on his own. His own pain. His own grief. Work kept the hurt firmly in its box where he never had to pay it any attention.

He'd been on his way home. Heading back for a shower, a change of clothes, maybe a quick four-hour nap. Then he'd planned on coming back to work.

But then he'd seen this woman climbing up a wobbly ladder, a ladder she should never have been up in the first place, on her own. He'd seen her reaching out for things that she hadn't got a chance in hell of reaching.

He'd seen how badly it had wobbled and he'd dropped his own briefcase and caught her, feeling the weight of her fall into his arms. He'd looked into her eyes up close, those pools of liquid brown, flecked with gold and green, and had felt a smack of something hard in his gut.

He'd intended to give her a dressing-down there and then. To yell at her for being so stupid and complacent, but in the fall her long hazelnut hair had come loose of its clip and lain over his arm, soft and silken, and it had taken a moment for him to realise that he'd been staring at her for much too long and that he really ought to let her go. The way you let go of a dangerous animal before it could bite or sting you.

She'd been unthinking in her actions. She'd assumed she would be okay, that somehow the rules didn't apply to her, and she'd been wrong.

Her beauty had thrown him briefly. There had been a second, maybe two, in which he'd momentarily been stunned by those chocolate eyes of hers, but then he'd cast those distracting thoughts to one side.

So she was attractive. So what? Beauty counted for nothing in his department. He needed solid workers. Excellent nurses. Team players. People who played by the rules. Not lone rangers who thought the whole world ought to revolve around them.

She'd blushed, looked embarrassed and had glanced down and away from him. His insides had twisted at her sweetness, flipping and tumbling like an acrobat in the Cirque du Soleil and the sensation had so startled him that he'd almost been unable to speak.

Offering to help her with the tree had seemed logical. Gentlemanly. A way for him to gather his thoughts and re-actions. To make sure she stayed safe. And give him time to put his own walls back up.

But it had been more than that. Exactly what, he

couldn't say. It had been a long time since a woman had disturbed him like that.

Not since Meredith...

He looked at the rest of Naomi's things dashed across the floor and started to pick them up again, trying to find places for them, trying to find order in the chaos.

He hadn't thought about Meredith for ages.

But that was a good thing surely. It meant he was moving on, didn't it? For too long, it had been a painful, persistent memory. When he'd thought of his wife, it had been about the days following the accident—sitting at her bedside in hospital, holding her hand, praying that she would wake, praying that she would recover. Holding out hope for her.

As the years had passed, the better memories of his time with Meredith had come to the fore. He was able to remember the good times they'd shared. Their happiness on their wedding day. Their love. The pain and grief was still inside would still torment him when he allowed it to, but it had taken on a different form recently.

His vow to never get involved with another woman, never to open his heart up to another, had held strong. He could never love another the way he'd loved his wife; it just wasn't possible.

Until now, he'd never had to doubt himself, or feel that that vow was threatened in any way.

Yet something about Naomi Bloom needled him. In the short time he'd known her, she'd practically demanded his attention, his protection, his help. He'd been forced to get involved. No decent man would have left her to fend for herself with Mick. No gentleman would have walked away from her after the burglary. When he'd found out she had nowhere to go, there'd been no other sensible option but to ask her to stay.

It would be difficult having her in his home. But he could stay out of her way. It would be all above board. She could have Meredith's old craft room that he'd turned into a spare bedroom during one mad weekend of decorating before he'd thought of what to do with his time and his life to cope with his grief.

One night to allow Naomi to get proper locks for her doors, better security. It was just about one colleague helping another. It was about being a decent human being.

One night only.

She opened her bedroom door and came out, lugging a heavy suitcase with her. He got up to take it from her and lifted it easily. 'A lot of clothes for one night!'

'I'd rather not leave anything here to be stolen. Just in case.'

'Is there anything else you want to take?'

'There was some paperwork, but I've packed that away. I'm ready to go.'

He nodded. 'I guess we'd better get going, then. Are you hungry? Would you like me to pick us up something to eat on the way home?'

'Oh! Well, only if you're eating, too. I don't want to get in your way or disrupt your routine any more than I already have.'

'You haven't disrupted me at all,' he said, picking up her case and heading for the front door, hoping she couldn't see the lie in his eyes.

They walked back to the hospital car park in silence. He put her suitcase in the boot of his car and then opened the passenger door for her. She looked surprised, smiled a thank you and then slid into the seat. He closed her door and walked round to his side, his mind going a mile a minute.

The only woman to have set foot in his home had been

Meredith and that was, of course, because she had lived there. Now he would be bringing home a stranger, a very attractive stranger, one who he hoped he could keep his distance from until she moved out. It ought to be easy, he thought. His penthouse flat was pretty large, and it was just one night.

If all else fails, I'll just put on my headphones and wear a blindfold.

Dr Williams's home was amazing. She'd never seen anything like it. She felt like Cinderella—going from her poor, ragamuffin lifestyle to this rich, sumptuous, stunning elegance that all seemed too much to take in.

His flat was on the top floor, not the bottom, like hers. The square footage must have been in the thousands and the space was open-plan, all glass windows, wooden floors and soft leather sofas. It had a minimalist element to it but looked nothing like what she'd expected from a single man. There were even fresh flowers on top of a grand piano in the corner of the living room.

He saw her notice them. 'My cleaner brings them in.'

She nodded, touching the long green stems. 'That's kind of her.'

'She insists. Tells me it brightens up the place. Makes it welcoming.' He didn't sound convinced.

'She's right.' Her fingers slid over the smooth black sheen of the piano. 'You play?'

He nodded. 'A little. You?'

She blew out a little puff of air. 'I could probably manage chopsticks if you reminded me how to do it.'

He smiled grimly, a darkness to his eyes. Was there pain there? Something… As if a part of him was missing. Or as if there was a part he was hiding, or at least trying to.

'You have a lovely home, Dr Williams.'

'Tom.'

She looked at him and smiled, feeling strange using his first name like that. 'Tom, okay.'

He looked about him as if seeing the flat for the first time. 'Let me show you to your room. Then you can settle, or I could make us something to eat. You must be hungry—it's been a long night.'

'You cook?'

'Yes.'

'From scratch?'

'Is there any other way?' He pulled up the handle on her suitcase and wheeled it across the floor behind him.

Naomi followed him down a corridor and through a door and suddenly she found herself standing in a bedroom that was as big as her whole flat. 'Wow. It's beautiful.'

'There's closet space…plenty of hangers. The bathroom is back through here; it's the door to your right.'

She followed him through the doorway into the bathroom and the light came on all by itself, controlled by a sensor. She smiled and glanced at her reflection in the mirror. She looked a mess! Her face was pale, yet blotchy and her hair all over the place, whereas Tom stood beside her, coolly detached, perfectly groomed.

Stepping out of the bathroom, she ran a hand through her hair in an effort to control it. 'I'll probably have a bath, if that's okay?'

'Sure.'

'Thank you, Tom. For everything. You've gone above and beyond today.' Her voice began to wobble as she spoke and she swallowed hard, forcing back the tears of gratitude. She hated crying when she didn't mean to, but sometimes it seemed like her body was just so overwhelmed by certain stressful situations that she couldn't stop herself.

But she would not cry in front of him again!

He simply smiled and backed away, most likely pleased to be escaping her tumultuous existence.

Naomi went back to the spare room and sank onto the bed, looking around her. What curious twist of fate had intervened in her life today? A new job. A burglary. And a soft place to fall. At least for tonight.

Sighing, she pulled off her coat and hung it up on the back of the door. She'd run herself a bath, maybe have a bite to eat and then hopefully she'd get a good night's sleep.

She didn't expect she would. It had been one heck of a day! And now she was suddenly living in her boss's home. That felt...odd. She didn't know him and the understanding he must have of her at this point was tenuous. He obviously didn't let people get too close. Everything about the man screamed 'keep away!' but he'd been generous and offered her a bed for the night when she'd had no other choice. That was good of him, right?

She was going to have to think of a way to thank him for this.

A huge thank you indeed.

Tom stood in his kitchen furiously whisking eggs for some omelettes. It felt strange knowing that he wasn't alone. That there was someone else in his home. A woman. A beautiful woman. And a work colleague, no less.

That would get the hospital grapevine going, no doubt. Especially if they arrived for work tomorrow together in his car. Perhaps he could let her get out at an earlier point?

He shook his head. Was he really that rude? Or worried about his reputation? Of course not. Everyone knew him at work. He was dedicated, honest, hard-working. No lad-about-town, causing outrageous rumours.

Besides, they might be lucky. No one might notice.

Naomi was in Merry's room. The room she had used

as a craft room, making cards, decoupage and that other thing she'd done…quilling? Or something like that. She'd been so talented at it. Sometimes he'd gone into that room to see what she was working on and had been amazed at this beautifully constructed hummingbird or peacock or mythical creature, all made out of coloured curls of paper. He remembered her smiling face looking up at him and saying, 'What do you think?'

And now Naomi was in there. Did she know? Could she sense it? He'd barely been able to stay in there and it had taken all his strength to redecorate it. To change it from what it had been. To take away the pain of the once pale blue walls.

They were a peach colour now. He'd not been in there since he'd painted it, except to change the bedding.

All the crafting stuff was gone, packed away. Some of it he'd given away. Instead, he'd installed a big wrought-iron bed in there along with bespoke beech furniture. It was all very plain. Simple. For guests. Not that he'd been expecting any guests. But if he gave the room a purpose, rather than it just lying empty, he could forget about his dreams for that room and what he'd once hoped it would turn out to be.

A nursery. Because one day, he and Merry would have tried to start a family. They'd talked about it anyway…

It would never be that now. And now it was Naomi's room. For one night anyway.

He tried to focus on the eggs, on grating cheese, on slicing courgettes and mushrooms, but his brain kept on torturing him with the image of her eyes, the way she'd looked up at him when he'd caught her falling from that ladder.

This was crazy! Why should it bother him what her eyes had looked like? Or that her skin had been smooth like porcelain, that her lips had looked full and soft? They were just work colleagues. Just associates. He was helping her out.

He whisked the eggs harder, trying not to think about her. He tried to focus on all the work he needed to get through tomorrow, but he could only envision her face and the way she'd felt in his arms...

Cursing, he put down the bowl of eggs and just stood still for a moment. Perhaps what he needed was a breather. A moment of mindfulness, to get himself back on track. He thought of the patients he'd seen that day. Their cases. The injuries. The treatments. The protocols.

Yes. That was working.

The door to the guest room opened and out walked Naomi in a thigh-length robe, with her hair all scooped up in a towel.

He quickly picked up the eggs and whisked them some more. 'Are you hungry?'

'I'm starving.'

'Good.' He tried not to breathe in all the aromas that she'd somehow brought out with her. There was a hint of lavender and something else sweet, warm and clean. She perched herself on a stool at his breakfast bar and he saw long, toned legs and dainty feet with pink-painted toenails. 'I'll make a start, then.'

'Can't wait.'

He swallowed hard and turned his back.

CHAPTER THREE

SHE WOKE WITH a start, a bad dream about smelly men in balaclavas still in her consciousness as she blinked quickly and looked about the strange room. Then she remembered.

Tom's.

She glanced at the clock on the bedside table. Five-forty-two a.m. It was early. But she had to be at work at seven, ready for the shift handover at seven-fifteen, so there didn't seem much point in trying to go back to sleep. She'd be getting up in twenty minutes anyway. Throwing off the covers, she got up and quickly made her bed, before getting dressed.

She moved quietly, hoping not to disturb Tom. She'd already put him out enough yesterday, especially last night when her presence had meant he couldn't even relax in his own home. The last thing she wanted was to wake him early and disturb his sleep pattern.

He was a good man, she thought. Despite the prickly exterior. He'd opened his home to a complete stranger, giving her the space she'd needed to just settle and breathe and get over her stressful day.

After their omelettes last night—which, due to something magical he'd done with Tabasco sauce and tomatoes, had been the most incredible she had ever tasted—he had wished her goodnight and disappeared to his room. She had watched him go, silent and strong, his long, lean figure moving gracefully like a cat into the shadows.

She'd taken the opportunity to look around his living space and discovered that Dr Tom Williams seemed very much a solitary man. There was no room for sentiment here. Each piece of furniture or decor had been chosen for its aesthetic appeal, rather than being some old family heirloom. There were no pictures on the walls of family or loved ones, no photo albums. Every surface was clean and uncluttered and only his bookshelves showed some hint to his character—clearly work focused, as all his books had been medical texts.

Was work all he thought about? She saw no sign of any other interest. There were no knick-knacks lying around like those she'd had all over the place. No personal touches. There was just the piano and, even then, she wondered if that was for him to play, or just another element of style. The only homely touch—the flowers—had been brought in by his cleaner.

But Naomi was thankful that he was focused on his work. Because apart from that small chat they'd had whilst he'd been preparing food in the kitchen, he had left her alone. He'd given her space, stayed out of her way.

It was his home and he was hiding in it. Perhaps he wasn't that thrilled to have her here after all? Perhaps he had felt compelled to suggest that she stay with him because he thought it was the gentlemanly thing to do. Tom certainly seemed like a gentleman, from the little she knew of him.

Still, she felt safe getting up this early and having a few minutes to herself before he surfaced. Perhaps she could make him a coffee and some toast, or cereal. She had no idea if he would be a cereal type of man. A quick look in his kitchen would tell her what she wanted to know. But it would be good to do something nice *for him* to show her appreciation. After all, later today she would be out of his hair.

She opened her bedroom door and was surprised to find all the lights on and Tom already up and about in his kitchen. He looked over at her. 'Good morning. Sleep well?'

She wasn't used to being greeted like that in the mornings, even when she'd been married. Back then, she'd fall sleep, exhausted, after a long, physical day and when she woke and went into her husband's room, the first words out of his mouth would usually be to tell her what sort of a night he'd had. Whether he'd got any sleep at all. There had been no *hellos*. No *good mornings*.

'I slept very well, thank you. You?'

'Seven hours. Can I get you anything? Coffee? Breakfast?'

She stood on the opposite side of the breakfast bar. 'I was going to make *you* breakfast. I didn't think you'd be up yet.' She saw he must have been up for quite a while— his hair was still slightly damp from the shower, the auburn a deeper red whilst it was wet, and his jawline was freshly shaved.

'What would you like?'

'Just toast for me.'

'Anything on it? Jam? Honey? Marmalade?'

'You have all of those?' She smiled.

'I do.'

She liked watching him in the kitchen. He seemed at home in it. 'Marmalade will be lovely.'

He cut two fresh slices from a large bloomer and popped the bread in the toaster, then poured her a coffee from a cafetière and passed her the milk and sugar.

'You're very domesticated, Dr Williams.'

He paused briefly to consider her words. 'Because I can make toast and pour coffee?'

'Because you know how to make someone feel welcome. I can appreciate it must be hard to have a stranger in your home, but you've made me feel like it's okay to be here, so…thank you.'

His ocean-blue eyes met her mocha brown just for a brief second. He gave a quick glance of gratitude, of appreciation and then looked away again, busying himself with the breakfast. 'Any idea of what you're going to do about your flat?'

He was changing the subject. She wondered if she'd made him uncomfortable. 'I don't know. I've got work first, so I guess I'll have to sort it out later.'

'Everywhere will be closed later. Why don't you take the day off?'

'On my second day? No chance. No, I'll just have to hope for the best. Find someone to fix the door somewhere…'

He looked torn, as if he had something to say, but couldn't say it.

The toast popped up and he handed it over on a plate, piping hot, along with a choice of marmalades, one with bits and one without.

'Oh…er…thank you.'

'It's no problem.'

She hoped he was telling the truth.

'Josephine McDonald?'

Her first patient of the day had already been seen by the triage nurse, who had noted on her card that earlier that day Josephine had misused her father's nail gun and had a six-inch nail shot through the end of her index finger.

Naomi looked out across the waiting room and watched

as a young woman stood up, grimaced and then walked over to her, clutching at her left hand that was wrapped up in a tea towel.

It was an impressive-looking nail.

'Let's take a look at that, shall we?' Naomi walked Josephine back to a cubicle and sat her down, pulling the curtain closed. 'So, how did this happen?' She took hold of her patient's hand, slowly turning it this way and that, to see what damage had been caused.

'I was helping my dad out with a job. He's a carpenter and he was letting me use the nail gun. I got…distracted… and somehow my finger ended up getting pierced.'

Naomi could understand. She was the accidental type, too. 'What distracted you?'

Josephine blushed. 'A guy.'

Naomi smiled at her patient. 'Oh. I see. Was he worth it?'

Josephine nodded enthusiastically. 'Oh, yes! Definitely!' She sighed dramatically. 'What can I say? A girl gets her head turned by a handsome man and *always* gets hurt.'

Naomi smiled again and checked for capillary refill on the girl's nail, which was fine, and stroked her finger. 'Can you feel this? And this?'

'Yes.'

'Good. I don't think there's any nerve damage. Can you bend the finger?'

'Yes. But I can feel it pulling on the nail.'

'We'll need an X-ray to make sure it's not gone through the bone and if you get the all-clear we can pull it out. Have you had a tetanus shot recently?'

Josephine blanched. 'I think so. Just a year or two ago. Pull it out? Won't that hurt?'

'We'll do a nerve block beforehand and you can suck

on some gas and air if you need it. Is your father with you? Someone to hold your hand?'

'Dad's in the waiting area.'

'Didn't you bring the hot guy with you?'

'Er...no. Apparently he doesn't do well with blood.'

'Right.' She smiled.

'What can you do? You see a hot guy, you have to give him the old "come hither" look. I just wasn't coordinated enough to be alluring *and* shoot a nail.'

Naomi smiled, trying to picture herself giving anyone a 'come hither' look. But then she stopped herself. Why would she do that? She wasn't looking for a relationship. She was happy being single and independent for a while. This was her first foray into the world alone, without her mother sticking her oar in, or without having to consider her husband's needs. She was finally free to do as she pleased.

'It's not bleeding, so let's get you round to X-ray.' She turned in her chair, reaching for the X-ray referral card, and filled in the details. 'Take this—' she handed it over and reopened the cubicle curtain '—and head straight down, follow the red line on the floor, round to the right and past the second set of chairs. Put the card in the slot and they'll call you through when they're ready.'

'Thanks.'

She watched the patient walk away and then started to clean down the cubicle. They hadn't really used it, but she stripped the bed of its paper sheet, wiped it down with clinical cleansing wipes and redid the sheet. As she did so the cubicle curtain next to hers was whipped open. 'Dr Williams!'

Was her heart beating just a little faster than normal? It definitely felt that way. She took a steadying breath to calm herself and inwardly gave herself a dressing-down.

There was no need to get nervous with the man. He was
her boss, yes, but that was all he was. She'd be moving
out of his flat later.

'Nurse Bloom.'

He dismissed his patient, who hobbled away on newly
acquired crutches, and then he turned back to smile at her.
He looked very dashing today in his dark navy trousers
and matching waistcoat against a crisp white shirt. She
had to admit she did like a man that dressed well. Vincent
had always worn quite loose-fitting clothes like tracksuit
bottoms and T-shirts. They had been the easiest things to
dress him in and he'd liked to feel comfortable whilst in
his wheelchair. So to see a man who knew how to dress
well, who took pride in his appearance, without being vain,
was a nice thing to see and enjoy.

'The department looks decidedly less Christmassy
today.'

She laughed good-naturedly. 'Yes. There should be
hearts going up soon, in readiness for Valentine's.' She
blushed slightly at the inference she'd made that it was
time for hearts and romance. Her mind scrabbled to redi-
rect their conversation. 'Or perhaps eggs for Easter? I'm
sure the shops have them already.'

'You like to celebrate all the holidays?'

Naomi shrugged as she walked alongside him back to
the central desk where a lot of the staff filled in paperwork
or checked information on the computer. 'Well, I like the
chocolate aspect. Is that wrong?'

'Absolutely not. In fact, I think it's almost law.' He sat
down at the desk, opened his file and started writing his
notes.

She noted his hands. He had fine hands, with long fingers, like a pianist's. So, perhaps he did play that beautiful instrument in his home. He wore a simple band on his

middle finger, which might have been tungsten, or platinum. It looked as if it could be a wedding band, but it was on the wrong digit.

It's none of my business.

Irritated with her own response to that thought, Naomi picked up the next card from triage and glanced at it. It was a child with a head wound. As she went to leave she heard Tom's voice call her name.

'Nurse Bloom?'

Turning, she looked at him, admiring the strong line of his jaw, the flicker of muscle as he clenched and unclenched it, as if he were debating with himself. 'Yes?'

'When you have a moment…when you have a break, would you come and find me? There's something I'd like to run past you.'

Run past me?

'Have I done something wrong?' She frowned, not knowing what it could be and worried that she might be in trouble again already. Now her heart really *was* pounding in her chest.

'No. Just…something personal. That's all.'

'Oh. Okay.'

Something personal.

That's all.

She wondered what it could be. Maybe she'd done something she shouldn't have done back at his flat. Had she left something out of place? Not put the lid back on the toothpaste, or something? He might be picky about things like that. It had certainly been neat. Everything in its place…

Worried, she headed back to the waiting room and called her next patient.

After she'd seen the child with the head injury, Naomi dealt with an elderly lady with a bad chest infection, then a sprained wrist and after that a young man with a build-up of blood behind his fingernail that needed releasing. Whilst she treated them all, she worried about what it was that Tom was going to ask her.

Something personal.

If it had nothing to do with work, then what could it be? He knew nothing about her, really. She'd made her bed in the flat. She'd cleaned up after herself, and been the perfect guest, hopefully. As her break time arrived she let the sister know she was going and then she began to look for Tom, her stomach in knots, her mouth dry.

She did *not* need complications. She'd had enough of those to last a lifetime. This was the start of her *new* life. She'd moved away from her old one and had come here to London, to the city, to prove to herself that she was independent and strong and could live her own life, with her own rules. This was her chance to be free of routine and stress. To only have to worry about herself.

Maybe he was going to ask her to make sure she moved out by the end of the day. She hoped not. After a full day shift until four p.m., she'd be lucky to have time to get back to her flat on St Bartholomew's Road and then find someone to fix her door, or a locksmith to add locks. She also wondered how much it would all cost. She didn't have bags of money and the small amount of savings she did have was meant to go towards a deposit on a better place. It wasn't supposed to pay for repairs to an old flat she didn't even like!

Tom was at the doctors' desk when she finally found him.

'Tom. I'm on my break now.' She fidgeted with the pens in her top pocket and straightened her fob watch.

'Let's grab a coffee and a bite to eat.'

He walked her up to the cafeteria and bought both of

them a cappuccino. He ordered a grilled breakfast for himself and when he asked her what she wanted she just shook her head. 'You've got to have something.' He placed a yoghurt and a banana onto his tray and, once he'd paid for it, they settled down at a table.

'You're probably wondering what this is about?'

She smiled and watched him tuck into his food with gusto. It did smell delicious and she tried to ignore the gorgeous scent of bacon and what smelt like pork and leek sausage as she opened her peach yoghurt. 'You've got me curious.'

'I want to help you.'

She sat in the seat opposite, staring at him, waiting for the axe to fall. 'Okay.'

'In the interests of my wanting the department to run smoothly, I'd like you to feel you could stay at my place. For an extra day or two whilst you get your flat sorted.'

'Stay? I thought—'

'It's not ideal, I know, but I've been thinking about your situation and I would feel remiss if you felt that you had to leave when your circumstances aren't exactly sorted.'

She blushed. Wow. She had not been expecting that. 'That's very generous of you, Tom. Thank you.'

He sipped his coffee. 'Not generous. I'm just being practical.'

Practical. Right.

Tom saw her face change. The uncertainty and nervousness that had been there a moment before dissipated and surprise and relief manifested themselves instead.

He'd almost been as surprised about the offer himself. If someone had asked him yesterday whether he'd have taken in a waif or stray, he would have said no. If someone had asked him if he would then have offered that beautiful young woman the chance to stay in his own home for a few more days he would have said they were crazy.

Last night he'd felt uncomfortable with her being there. He'd made as little interaction as he could get away with without being rude. But he'd looked out for her, cooked for her, talked to her a little and had found himself intrigued. He was interested by this woman whom he'd suddenly acquired in his department and in his life.

Not that he was interested in her in *that way*. There was no point in pursuing that. There was only ever one true love, one true soulmate for a person, and he'd already met his, even if she had been taken from him too soon. Meredith had been killed in a tragic accident that had taken her from him before they'd even had their first full year of marriage. His heart had truly belonged to her and now he kept it locked away, safe and protected from the outside world where cruel things happened and people in love were tormented. No, there were going to be no more women for Tom Williams.

They were off-limits. Even if last night he'd been plagued with thoughts of Naomi in the next room. He'd lied to her about getting that good night's sleep. He should have had seven hours. But instead, he'd lain in his bed, thinking about her, seeing those long legs that had emerged after her bath, gazing into those eyes of hers that he couldn't bear to look at for longer than a second in case she saw the *interest* in his own eyes. Oh, and the way that she laughed. The way her whole face lit up with genuine joy when she did.

So he couldn't allow himself to think about Naomi. She was everything that went against his self-imposed rules. But he *could* help her with her living situation.

'This is so unexpected.'

He nodded. 'Yes. But expecting you to get your place sorted in one night seems both impossible and impractical. St Bartholomew's Road? It's not a nice place. I'm sorry. I'm not normally judgemental, but you seem to deserve…better.'

'And I can stay at yours for the next few days?'

'Yes.'

'I can't believe it! That's so sweet of you. Are you sure? Don't you want to know more about me? I mean, I could be a crazy axe murderer, or something.'

'I know enough. And if you handled an axe on a regular basis, I'm sure you'd be missing a limb or something by now, from what I've seen so far. My place is big enough for us both to be able to do our own thing. We won't get in each other's way. And then, with a few days' grace, you can find a better flat. Something more suitable.'

'Less rough, you mean?'

'Less…challenging.' He smiled at her quickly, then looked away. He'd been thinking hard about this all morning. Did he really want to do this? Could he really open up his home to a stranger? It had already been odd having her there in Meredith's old room. It had been strange knowing she was there doing whatever it was that women did when they spent ages in the bathroom, but…he could arrange it for them so they had different shift patterns so that they wouldn't be running into each other all the time.

Naomi sat forward and this time sipped her drink, thinking carefully. 'Why do you want to help me?'

Because I can't get you out of my head and the idea of you living in that dump terrifies me.

'Because I think anyone would deserve better.' He couldn't tell her it was because he'd actually quite liked seeing her there this morning. He'd liked having someone to talk to, even if it was only briefly, over breakfast. Normally, once he was dressed, he'd head straight out to work, not talking to another soul until he arrived.

This morning had been different and he'd found he liked it. It had been like it had when Meredith was around.
Meredith.

Was he doing something wrong? No. No, he wasn't. But why then did he suddenly feel so guilty, when he was only trying to be kind?

The sooner the next few days were over, the better.

Living in Tom's flat was beyond her wildest dreams. She never would have imagined herself in a place such as this and yet here she was.

Naomi stroked her fingers along the kitchen surfaces, smiling in appreciation at the clean, smooth lines of the beech woodwork and the frosted etched glass in some of the cupboard doors. It was a dream home and she was living in it! If only for a little while.

Her suitcase, which she'd only partially unpacked the night before, was now empty, and all her things were hanging in the wardrobe.

Tom had given her a lift home and he was getting changed, whilst she'd offered to cook for them both. Not that she was a great cook. Or any cook at all, truth be told. Most things she cooked came out of tins or packets. 'Add an egg' recipes were the most adventurous she usually got. She looked through his cupboards to see what she could use.

In the fridge there was a large steak. She could cut that into two and maybe make some mashed potatoes and he had fine beans and broccoli. She started peeling and chopping and soon had a couple of pans on the boil, as Tom came out into the living area. 'You're cooking?'

'I am. Steak.'

'Sounds good.'

He *looked* good. He'd changed into some black jeans

and a soft white fitted T-shirt, which showed off his beauti-fully toned arms to perfection. Who knew a chiselled god existed under the suit he normally wore at work?

'How do you like it?'

'Medium, please.'

She nodded. 'Good.' Now she was stuck. 'Er...how will I know when it's medium?'

Tom's face cracked into a near smile. 'Hold out your hand.'

Her hand? What did he want with her hand? She held it out and then watched as he modelled, using his index fin-ger to touch the fleshy pad beneath his thumb. 'The way the pad of flesh under your thumb feels? That would be what a raw steak feels like. Put your index and thumb to-gether. Feel it now? That's well done.'

She watched him and focused, replicating his actions with her own, marvelling at how the different parts felt.

'Now press your ring finger and thumb together. That pad is now medium.'

Naomi did them all again. 'That's brilliant!'

'I'm glad you like it. Now you'll know.'

'Now I'll know,' she repeated, picking up the broccoli and rinsing it under the tap. 'There is something I *don't* know.'

'What's that?'

'How well you actually play that piano over there.' She nodded in the direction of the piano and watched his face.

A strange mix of emotions passed over it and his eyes clouded slightly. If she had blinked, she'd have missed it, but she saw it happen. Something about playing the piano had caused a bad memory.

'I haven't played for a long time.'

'No? Why not?' She knew she shouldn't press him, but

she was curious. Surely anyone who had such a beautiful instrument would play it as often as they could?

'Because I only ever played it for my wife.' Naomi watched as regret and grief filled his face and then he swept away from her and disappeared back to his room.

She stood in the kitchen, her hands pausing in their actions, her mouth slightly open. She hadn't known he was married.

But then…she remembered the ring on his finger. The wedding band.

I did know. I did! And now I've upset him.

She felt so foolish. It was only their second night together and she'd already ruined it. She'd upset her host, reminding him of a past he quite clearly didn't want to remember. Putting down the knife, she wiped her hands on a cloth and walked to his room, her knuckles raised ready to rap on the wood.

Only she paused.

Did she know him well enough to have an in-depth chat? Was it her place to pry into events he clearly didn't want to share? If he had wanted to talk to her about it, he wouldn't have gone to his room.

Clearly she shouldn't knock. Her hand lowered. Feeling redundant, she went back to the kitchen, her footsteps slow and heavy. Maybe he didn't want to discuss his wife and whatever might have happened there, but she could cook him an amazing steak and mash.

Well, I'll have a go anyway. Surely I can't get this wrong?

She turned on the small kitchen television and dropped the steaks into the sizzling oil.

Tom paced in his room. What the hell was he doing? Why had he reacted like that? What was he, twelve?

And what's that smell?

Feeling ridiculous, he yanked open the bedroom door, ready to apologise for his behaviour to Naomi, only to notice the kitchen area was filled with smoke and the smell of burning, his fire alarm suddenly squawking into life.

'What the…?' He rushed forward to see Naomi, gasping, flicking a towel at a burning pair of steaks, screaming every time she fanned the flames to even greater heights. 'Stop!' He pushed past her, turning off the gas, grabbed the tea towel and lowered it slowly over the flames, so that they were dowsed in an instant.

Naomi was coughing and spluttering. 'I'm so sorry! I don't know what happened.'

Tom grabbed another towel and began wafting it beneath the fire alarm, until he'd cleared away enough smoke for it to stop. Once silence reigned again and the alarm could only be heard as some sort of ghostly sound in their ears, he turned to her and raised his eyebrows in question.

'I'm so sorry, Tom. There was a cooking show on and they poured alcohol into the pan and tipped it somehow to…'

'Flambé?'

'Yes and it kind of worked.'

'Too well. How much alcohol did you put in there?'

'A splash.'

'Hmm.'

'I'm so sorry. I've never done it before and I so wanted to impress you with a good steak, after I upset you earlier…'

His face clouded over. 'It's okay. No one got hurt. Except the steaks.' He peered at the blackened bits of meat, so totally beyond rescue. To Naomi's surprise and disbelief pretty soon he was smiling, then laughing. She couldn't help but laugh, too, thrilled and delighted at how the expression lit up his entire face. It was as if he hadn't laughed properly in a long time.

When she got her breath back, she slumped onto one of the kitchen stools. 'You must think I'm a disaster area.'

He slid onto one of the stools beside her. 'A little. How on earth have you survived all these years?'

Her cheeks flamed. 'I became best friends with a microwave and meals where you only had to pierce lids before cooking.'

He smiled and shook his head. 'Has no one ever taught you to cook?'

She shook her head. 'My mother wasn't the best at passing on her skills. She didn't really have any, except for falling in love with the most unsuitable men she could find.'

He stared at her for a moment longer than was comfortable. Despite her hazardous skills in the kitchen and her total inability to not fall off ladders, he *liked* her. She was innocent and sweet and funny.

Don't.

Images of Meredith instantly flooded his mind and he felt guilty. Admiring another woman was wrong. He needed to think of something else. He shouldn't be thinking that it should be Merry standing with him in this kitchen, instead of Naomi. He pushed the guilty thoughts away. 'I'll teach you how to cook.'

'What?'

'I'll teach you.'

'But you've already saved me. Rehomed me. You don't have to turn me into a Michelin-starred chef, too.'

He picked up the pan with the charred remains and tipped it into the bin. 'Yes. I do. If we're going to survive this week.'

She sighed and smiled her thanks. 'Right. So…veg and mash?'

'There might be some fish fingers in the freezer.'

'I can manage those.'

He nodded in approval. 'Excellent. I'll await your culinary delights, forthwith.'

He laid the table and she brought over their steaming hot plates, laying one down in front of him.

It felt good to be serving someone a meal again. To sit down and just share that moment. They were simple pleasures. Even though she'd been looking forward to being free of all of that, to spending time alone, she suddenly found herself craving the company. 'I haven't done this in a long time.'

He looked up. 'Eaten fish fingers?'

She smiled. 'Shared a meal. It's good. You forget what that's like.'

He looked pensive, then he smiled back. 'Yeah.'

She pushed her broccoli around her plate, then patted the mash, sculpting it with her fork. She wanted to make him feel better, after she'd annoyed him earlier with that comment about his piano. Perhaps if he knew that she'd been through marriage and a loss, too, it would help. 'I was married, too, not so long ago.'

Tom took a drink of his water and met her gaze across the table.

'His name was Vincent and we were married for eight years.'

'Long time.'

'It was. Some days it seemed longer than that. Only afterwards, did I realise how short it actually was.'

Tom speared a piece of his broccoli. 'You don't have to tell me what happened, if you don't want to.'

But she did want to share it with him. If they were going to be sharing a flat, she saw no reason not to share with him part of her past. Besides, she thought he might be interested—in a medical sense. 'Fibrodysplasia ossificans progressiva happened.'

His fork stopped halfway to his mouth. 'Stone Man Syndrome? That's rare. Only about one person in every two million gets it.'

'Have you ever seen a case?'

'No.'

'Vincent had issues from a young age. It was noted when he was a baby that he had these deformed toes, but no one made the connection until later. At first it was bone growths in his neck and shoulders. When I met him, he was already in a wheelchair, confined to a sitting position, and he was in and out of hospital with pneumonia and lung infections.'

'It must have been difficult for you both.'

'It's hard to see someone you love become imprisoned within their own body, their own skeleton turning on them. The slightest injury caused another bone growth.'

Tom put down his knife and fork, totally focused on her story.

'I left work to become his full-time carer.'

'I'm sure he was an amazing man.'

She nodded. 'He was. Upbeat. Positive. As much as he could be until the end. He had his dark days, though.'

'Don't we all?' He looked down at the tablecloth. 'I'm sorry for your loss.'

She smiled and pushed away her plate. 'I managed not to burn the house down anyway. That was a bonus!' She picked up their plates and took them away into the kitchen, scraping the remains of the meal into the bin. It hadn't been the best thing she'd ever cooked, but it would do.

Tom came into the room and poured them both a glass

of wine. 'And what did you do to relax? When you weren't looking after your husband?'

She clinked her glass to his. 'Reading. Researching his disease. Looking for treatments, looking for medical trials. Anything that could help him.'

'And what did you do *for you*?'

'Me?' she asked, surprised by the question. 'I can't remember.'

He stared at her. Then he sipped his wine, thoughtfully.

CHAPTER FOUR

Tom found the next week difficult. It was harder than he'd imagined. He'd thought it would be a simple task of scheduling Naomi to work days and putting himself on late shifts or nights, so that he wouldn't be always in her space, or she in his, but somehow wherever he went, there were reminders—her perfume, her toothbrush in the bathroom, her little make-up bag sitting on the counter. And the times when they *did* find themselves at home or at work at the same time were even harder.

Once he came back to a darkened flat in the middle of the night, expecting her to be asleep. She had been. Only she'd fallen asleep on the sofa, with the television still playing, and he'd stood over her for a minute, just watching her sleep, her face so relaxed and peaceful. Then he'd felt guilty for watching her, aware she could have woken and found him standing there. So he'd hurried to his room and closed the door, lying on his bed and praying for sleep.

When he'd first met her, he'd been determined not to like her. But then he'd seen at work what a great nurse she was, what fabulous rapport she could achieve with even the most difficult of patients and at home...at home, she would make sandwiches for him and leave him notes pinned to the fridge, so he knew where to find them. She'd even attempted to bake some cookies one night and thankfully hadn't burned the place down in doing so. They'd been a little tough on the teeth, but he'd eaten them anyway, because she'd tried so hard.

She'd even made progress with getting her flat sorted. A few of their work colleagues knew people who knew other people and the plyboard door had been replaced with an old interior one. Her locks had been changed and she'd even had time to go over there and straighten the place up a bit.

Now, Tom had one more day with her before the 'few days' they'd talked about were up and he didn't know how he felt about that. For some reason he was a bit short-tempered with everyone. Irritable.

Tom and Naomi were both working in Resus, when an ambulance arrived with their first patient of the shift. She was an elderly woman, who was thin and frail with liver-spotted hands and patchy grey hair. Her pale pink nighty, edged with a thin line of lace, looked much too large for her tiny body.

The paramedic wheeled the patient into position. 'This is Una Barrow, eighty-nine years of age and a resident of Tall Oaks Care Home.' Tall Oaks was a residential home for patients with Alzheimer's. 'The care staff there grew concerned when she stopped eating and drinking yesterday and today she's got a temperature of thirty-eight point two, sats of ninety-three per cent and a blood pressure of ninety over sixty, which is usual for her. She wouldn't allow us to do a blood-sugar reading, she became combative and, due to her friable skin and past history of osteopenia, we didn't think it was worth the risk of injuring her. Hope that's okay, doc?'

Tom nodded. That was fine. They could get a blood-sugar reading for her here easily enough. 'Sure. Any other medical history?'

'Nothing of significance.'

'Family?'

'She has a daughter, but she lives over a hundred miles away. We got Tall Oaks to give her a ring and I believe she's on her way.'

Right. So it was best to try and get Una settled and sorted before the daughter arrived and then, hopefully, he would have good news to pass on.

'Okay, everyone, let's have a full top-to-toe assessment, please.'

He stood back, watching, listening, assessing, as his team, including Naomi, read out test results and observations. All obvious signs pointed to a urinary tract infection, but he'd need a urine sample to confirm the diagnosis.

Naomi was trying to get the blood sugar when suddenly Una clutched Naomi's hand.

'Rosie?' the elderly woman asked in a tremulous voice, staring off into the void.

'No, Una. I'm Naomi. A nurse. I'm here to look after you.' She gave the patient's hand a gentle squeeze, but Una tightened her grip and wouldn't let her go.

'Don't leave me, Rosie! They're trying to kill me!'

Tom watched as Naomi glanced back at him, signalling resignedly that she couldn't help with the assessments whilst the patient had a good firm hold of her hand.

He stepped forward. 'Una? I'm a doctor here and you're not in Tall Oaks any more. You're in hospital.'

Una blinked and focused on Tom's voice, her glazed eyes sliding from Naomi's face to his. 'Hospital?'

'That's right. You're safe. No one here will harm you, but you're not very well, Una. You've got a temperature and so we're going to make you feel better.'

She looked back to Naomi. 'Don't leave me here, Rosie.'

Tom glanced at Naomi and they shared a look. Alzheimer's was such a cruel disease, deftly taking away each and every day another small part of who someone was, often leaving them confused or frightened or, even worse, lucid, so that they had moments of knowing exactly what was happening to them. It was just as Naomi had faced with Vincent, those years and years of slowly losing someone.

Tom had also sat and watched Meredith slip away day by day. Luckily, she hadn't known what was happening to her.

But *he* had. He'd sat at the side of her bed, holding her lifeless hand, begging and praying that she would come back to him, and each day the doctors had reported a drop in her condition until those final, painful reports had indicated that she was to all intents and purposes brain-dead. By the end she'd only been kept alive by the ventilator. He and Meredith's parents had decided to turn off the machine keeping her alive, but it had been a horrible time, a horrible decision. Something he wouldn't wish on anyone. Just as he wouldn't wish Alzheimer's on anyone.

Tom caught Naomi's gaze, then spoke quietly. 'Let her think you're Rosie until the daughter gets here. It might make her feel better. Safer. We can get her blood sugar and urine sample from her if she's calm and relaxed.'

Naomi nodded, understanding. 'Okay. I'm here. It's all right.'

'Oh, my Rosie!' Una held Naomi's hand close to her chest and closed her eyes, seemingly more calm.

Naomi reached out to pull a plastic chair towards the side of the bed. Sinking into it, she smiled at Tom. 'She's got me held tight. I won't be escaping soon, I don't think.'

'That's okay. Hopefully the real Rosie will get here soon. Can you keep an eye on her? And note down her obs half-hourly?'

'Only because my writing hand is still free.' She

grabbed the patient's file, opening it and filling in what she could.

As Una's breathing deepened and she drifted off to sleep a male nurse, Stefan, came into Resus. 'Oh, Naomi…if only you'd hold *my* hand so intently!' Stefan was a dreadful flirt who, Tom knew, tried it on with most of the women in the hospital.

His skin prickled at the way he flirted so openly with Naomi.

Why should I let it bother me?

He stood over by the desk filling in his report at the computer station, keeping a subtle eye on them both.

Naomi simply smiled. 'I don't think it's your hand you want me to hold, Stefan,' she replied calmly, staring down at Una, keeping her voice regulated and not doing anything to disturb the sleeping patient.

Stefan laughed, collected the sterile pack he'd come in for and then headed back to the double doors. 'Ah, you know me too well, sweet girl. But I guess I can't compete with Dr Williams here. My pigeon chest can't outdo his six pack, can it? Must be nice seeing that in the morning, eh?'

As Stefan pushed through the doors, leaving them swinging back and forth, Tom looked to Naomi in shock.

Were they the subject of gossip already? How on earth had that happened? Naomi had been staying at his place for less than a week and *he* hadn't told anyone. He wondered if she had. Maybe they had simply been spotted leaving and arriving together on the few days they'd worked the same hours.

A surge of irritability flooded through him and he almost snapped his pen in half. He hated gossip. It distorted everything. The grapevine probably had blown the whole innocent affair out of proportion. God only knew what they were saying!

But what he really didn't like was the idea that his reputation was being run through the mud. Or Naomi's for that matter. They were just flatmates. Plain and simple. And it was only a temporary arrangement, which should be ending soon. Her old flat was practically sorted anyway and she would be able to start looking for a new place in earnest.

'Naomi...have you told anyone about our arrangement?'

She shook her head, looking just as shocked as he felt. 'No.'

'Two plus two is going to equal five unless we put a lid on this.'

'It's just gossip. They'll soon get bored.'

'Will they? I think you're more optimistic than I am.'

Tom looked at Naomi, her hand still in the patient's tight grasp. She had a simple beauty, an elegant face with regal features. Tom wondered if she knew she could probably be a model if she wanted to be. She didn't seem to be aware of her looks. Her long brown hair was always loosely gathered up into a clip and it never looked as if she'd spent hours styling it, but *still* it always looked amazing, soft and silken, deftly pulled this way and that, held in place by a pin or two. She wore no jewellery that he'd noticed, but she didn't need it. There was enough sparkle and colour in her eyes alone. Those deep chocolate pools captured him every time she looked at him. She had a very small beauty mark on her right cheek and soft, full pink lips. When she smiled, the effect it had on his insides was, simply put, devastating. He hated to admit it to himself but he was being pulled in by her lure.

Stefan and any of the other gossipmongers would have a field day with their idle rumours. It just wouldn't occur to them that the relationship he had with Naomi was completely innocent and above board. Surely anyone would take one look at Naomi's gorgeous good looks and assume that he would be trying to seduce her. They wouldn't assume anything else.

And I don't want to enforce their rumours.

He needed to try and create some space away from her and stop the rumour mill in its tracks. Asking her to stay had been a terrible decision.

'Any luck with flat-hunting?' He knew it was an abrupt change of subject and in direct contradiction of what he'd said to her the other day. Maybe he'd made a mistake. Maybe he shouldn't have encouraged her to get comfy and put her feet beneath his table. He really ought to be helping her to find a place to live. Then he could have his sanctuary back. His private place. His home. A place only for him and his memories.

'Um…no, nothing suitable yet.' She looked a little stunned by his change of topic and, although he felt guilty for making her feel that maybe she wasn't as welcome as she'd previously thought, he reminded himself that this was about self-preservation.

He didn't need complications in his life. Work was where he came to forget. It was the place where he thrived, where he felt safe, and if he couldn't feel that in the hospital, if it became yet another place where he felt uncomfortable, then he had no idea how he would survive.

'You might be needed in Majors, Nurse Bloom. Release yourself from the patient and go and check with them next door, please.' He knew he was being abrupt and he hated himself for it.

She looked up at him as if puzzled, but then she nodded and turned back to Una to see if she could slip her hand away, unnoticed.

She finally managed it. Stepping away, she quietly slid

Una's file into the space at the bottom of her bed. 'Who'll do her obs?'

'I will.'

'Okay. If you're sure.' When she disappeared through the doors, leaving him alone in Resus, he ran his fingers through his hair in exasperation and let out a heavy sigh.

What on earth was going on inside his head?

Majors had enough staff, but just as she was about to go back to Resus, Naomi saw a middle-aged woman walking through the department, looking lost and confused. 'Can I help you?' she asked.

The woman suddenly looked relieved to be able to share her burden. 'Yes! Please. I got called by my mother's care home to say she'd been brought here. Una Barrow? I asked at Reception and they sent me in here, but I think I've got a little lost.'

'It's a big department. It happens all the time. But follow me—I know where your mum is.'

'How is she?'

'Stable at the moment. We think she may have a urinary tract infection.'

'Oh, not again! But she's all right?'

'She's sleeping at the moment.' Naomi led the way into Resus, catching Tom's shocked expression at her returning so soon, but then his face registered relief when he saw she was with someone else. 'Tom? This is Una's daughter.'

'Rosie?' He came over to shake the woman's hand.

'Yes. Rosemary Sanders.'

'She's been asking for you.' He walked with her over to the patient and watched as she took her mother's hand. 'Your mother was brought into us with a high temperature, which we're slowly getting down. We've given her a paracetamol IV as well as a standard drip to keep her hydrated and to give the trimethoprim.'

'What's that?'

'It's an antibiotic. It works in about eighty per cent of these sorts of cases.'

'And what if that doesn't work?'

'We'll try a cephalosporin treatment.'

'Well, you sound like you know what you're doing.' She smiled at her mother. Una stirred and opened her eyes, spotting her daughter. 'Rosie…'

'Hello, Mum.'

Naomi stepped away to stand with Tom. 'Are you okay?'

He looked down, pulling a pen from his pocket and scribbling something on a scrap piece of paper. 'I'm fine. Why do you ask?'

She shrugged. 'You seem…upset.' She held his gaze and though he wished to tear his eyes away, he found, yet again, that he couldn't. 'If it's because I'm still at yours, it's just because I haven't found anywhere I can afford yet, and—'

'Would you check the stocks in the trolleys, please?' He could feel his heart pounding heavily in his chest and so he sat down to catch his breath. He suddenly wished she would move away from him, so he could think straight. He cursed himself for being horrible once again, but he didn't know what else he could do.

'Certainly. But only if you're all right.'

He laughed—a cynical, forced laugh. 'Why wouldn't I be all right?'

'I don't know.'

She looked at him, her face a mask of concern, and it was all he could do to ignore it. How did she have such an ability to affect him? It wasn't as if he'd been stranded in the desert, where there were no women, and she'd been the first one he'd seen when he got back to civilisation. He was surrounded by women all of the time. Why was *she* any different and how could *she* make him feel like his insides were all twisted? Like his blood were running hotter than normal? And those rumours... He couldn't stand people talking about him. He'd been the subject of gossip once before when Meredith had died and he'd come straight back into work the next day. People had gossiped then, whispering in corners, making judgements.

It irritated him. He was used to being calm and in control. Even when there was a dramatic event in Resus he could stay calm and focused.

But he couldn't with her around. Perhaps he could help her find somewhere. He could look a little harder. He'd really not done anything to help her find a new flat. Apart from providing a roof over her head whilst she looked. She'd had work to do and her old flat to sort out, so she could get her deposit back and...

He sighed. She was more in his space than he'd realised. And he wasn't ready for that. Not now. Not ever. He had to stop feeling this attraction to Naomi.

There couldn't be a future in it.

Naomi was in the staffroom on her morning break, feeling content. The days had flown by. She'd been living with Tom for a few weeks now, trying and failing to find her feet and a new flat. Although there'd been a few awkward moments between them since that day when Stefan had alerted them to the hospital gossip, it seemed to be going quite well. As colleagues, they'd worked together, mostly like a finely tuned engine. As flatmates, she had mostly felt welcome, and only on occasion had she got the feeling Tom was uncomfortable with her being there.

Valentine's Day, for instance, had been odd. With both

of them single, both of them trying not to reference the day, or the fact that they were both alone. She'd considered, briefly, sending him a joke card but common sense had told her that it wouldn't go down well, so they had both just worked as late as they could and grabbed a takeaway on the way home that night.

There were a few others in the staffroom, Stefan included, who sat chatting with his mates, laughing over a celebrity gossip magazine, whilst Naomi sat with a coffee and her new friend, Jackie.

Jackie was a healthcare assistant and they'd hit it off from day one. Naomi had immediately liked her because of her work ethic and ready smile. It seemed she knew everything about the department and she was always happy to point Naomi in the right direction if she needed it. But right now, Jackie was explaining to her about the Spring Ball.

'Are you going to go?'

Naomi shook her head. 'No.'

'You should. It's fabulous. Better than the Christmas party!'

'I wouldn't know. I probably won't go to that either.'

'Oh, you must go! It's fabulous. You get to dress up like a princess and dance with a handsome man. You could bring Dr Williams!'

Naomi tried to act confused. 'Why would I bring Dr Williams?'

'Because you're sleeping with him.'

What? 'No, I'm not! Is that what everyone's saying?' She felt her cheeks flame with heat.

Jackie leant in closer, lowering her voice. 'You've been leaving together. You arrive together. Everyone assumed—'

'They assumed wrong!' She got up and stormed over to the sink, unable to sit still for a moment longer. 'I got burgled. My place was trashed and Tom offered me a place to stay until I could arrange something else!'

Jackie held up her hands as if in surrender. 'Okay! I believe you! Whoa, calm down, woman. I'm only telling you what everyone is saying. We just thought…I mean, come on, he is delish!'

'He's a friend. A work colleague. My boss! Tom and I will be nothing more,' she said firmly and loudly, just as Tom walked in, holding his coffee mug.

He paused, glancing at her, his face impassive. He looked around at Jackie and the others all staring at him, waiting for him to say something, but he just went to the coffee pot and poured himself a refill and left again.

Naomi didn't realise she'd been holding her breath. She let it out, wondering how she would ever apologise to him for making them both the subject of so much gossip. Perhaps it would be wise to find a flat sooner, rather than later?

She sank down in the chair next to Jackie. 'Know anywhere I could live?'

Her friend stared back at her and shook her head. 'Sorry.'

She let out a sigh, wondering if everyone else's attempts at being strong and independent in the world came crashing down as badly as hers.

Tom stood outside the hospital clutching his mug of coffee and fighting the urge to march back into the staffroom.

He knew he wouldn't. He wasn't a violent man, or the confrontational type. But the urge to give everyone a piece of his mind had suddenly soared out of nowhere. Being the subject of idle gossip wasn't helping. He'd thought everyone had forgotten about all of that nonsense.

It was enough to make any man's blood boil.

I don't know why I'm getting so worked up about this!

She was just a work colleague. A tenant. A friend. An employee. Nothing more than that. And he didn't need her to be anything more than that, he reminded himself.

Naomi Bloom.

It all kept coming back to her! Nothing had been right in his life ever since she'd fallen from that stupid ladder into his arms.

Tom sat down on one of the benches and sipped his coffee. It wasn't too cold out. It was one of those rare February days when the sun shone brightly and there was no breeze, so it actually felt quite spring-like. Daffodils were coming up early and, above the light morning traffic, he could hear birdsong. It was almost a pleasant day, except…

It had been a day like this when Meredith had been hit by the car. The driver had been drinking and over the limit, but he'd also said the low sun had blinded him, blocking his view of another vehicle, causing him to swerve suddenly, mount the kerb and…hit Meredith.

She'd been jogging along the road, with her headphones in, music playing, and she'd not heard the rev of the engine, or the squeal of brakes before it was too late. Much too late.

He let out a heavy sigh. He had to be more vigilant. He couldn't involve himself with Naomi. Since her arrival in his life, he'd been disturbed, unable to concentrate, unable to sleep knowing that she was just in the next room. Now everyone was talking about them.

He didn't need that kind of reputation. He wanted everyone to think of him as a damned fine doctor and nothing else!

In the evening, Naomi was just starting to put together a quick meal. She'd put some pasta on to boil, had—admittedly—opened a carton of fresh tomato and basil sauce and was busy chopping up a fresh green salad. You couldn't burn salad. And she never went wrong with pasta. This was a good way to apologise to Tom for the day's events.

The radio was on and as she chopped she sang along to the music, not caring that she was off-key or didn't know half the words.

She had just reached for a handful of fresh herbs, when she noticed Tom had silently emerged from his room and was watching her dance and bop to the music. She blushed. 'Hi.'

Tom stood there, a slight smile of amusement on his face. 'Cooking again?'

Self-consciously, she patted her hair, realising the wispy loose bun was still held in place by the pencil she'd used earlier. She pulled it out, shaking her hair loose with her fingers as her cheeks coloured. She glanced down at the chopped salad leaves, the mix of rocket, radicchio and watercress. 'Erm, yes. But I'm certain we'll get through this one with the minimum amount of fuss.'

'No fire trucks?'

She laughed. 'No. Well… I hope not. Look, about today, Tom, I'm really sorry—'

'There's no need.' He held up his hands. 'It's fine. I should have known. I reacted badly to it, too. I was rude ignoring you and that was very wrong of me. I'm sorry.'

He looked it, too. She found herself feeling odd about it. Discomfited. When she'd had fallings-out with Vincent, they would apologise and she would hug him, gently, so as not to cause him injury. Injury only turned to more bone, but she had never stopped giving him hugs. She was that kind of person.

But to hug Tom? That wouldn't feel right. She didn't feel that she *had* the right to do that yet.

'I'm sorry, too. All you've done is look out for me

since you've known me and now I'm dragging your name through the mud.'

'I've been in worse. Mud is nothing, compared to some places you could be.'

She thought maybe he was referring to her experience with Vincent. Yes, that had been tough, watching someone die and not being able to do a thing about it. She'd felt the same sadness with the elderly patients with Alzheimer's. She understood how horrible it was to see a disease slowly picking away at a person, like a vulture, feeding on their soul, feeding on *who they were*. 'I agree.'

'I hope I haven't made you feel that you have to find another place sooner, rather than later.'

'I did feel that a little.'

'I'm sorry. But when Jackie implied today that we were…' he swallowed '…sleeping together, I just felt like they were all disregarding the feelings I had for my wife. I loved her so much and to lose her like that, in such a terrible accident… There should never be rumours like that about us. About me. I won't ever date. Not again.'

'Never?'

He shook his head. 'I've had my one true love. You don't get that a second time.'

She looked at him carefully. 'You believe there's only ever one true love for a person? That out of all the billions of people on this planet, we only ever have one person who could be our soulmate?'

He considered her words. 'It would be a miracle if there were another.'

'But in believing that, you're tying yourself to a lonely future. I loved Vincent, but I don't think he'll be my *only* love. I have to believe that there's more.'

'Maybe we're both right. But I won't have gossip about us. We have to set everyone straight.'

'All right.'

'And I'd like to help you look for a place. A *good* place. I can use my contacts.'

Clearly he still wanted to get rid of her. Disappointment filled her. 'I appreciate that, Tom.'

He looked as if he was going to say something else, but then he seemed to think better of it. Instead, he just smiled and went over to sit on the sofa.

The pasta was about to boil over. She caught it just in time and turned down the heat.

Disaster averted.

CHAPTER FIVE

THE DOORS FLEW open as the paramedics wheeled in their next patient. Tom, Naomi and the rest of the team all took a grip and helped transfer the patient from the trolley onto the flat bed.

Tom and Naomi had spent the last week or so flat-hunting but it hadn't gone well. Places had been either too small, or too far from work, bearing in mind that she would have to use buses or trains to get to Welbeck and the London traffic was notoriously bad.

They'd gotten into a routine. Work, eat, flat-hunt, sleep. It was a routine. A *safe* routine. Tom knew that just by concentrating on those few things, he could keep the topic of conversation away from the more dangerous areas. He didn't want to reveal too much of himself and he frequently felt that he was constantly warding Naomi off from asking personal questions.

The paramedic handed Tom the job notes.

'This is Derek, forty-two, he was involved in a car-versus-lamp-post incident approximately thirty minutes ago. The car was travelling at an estimated forty miles an hour and he swerved and hit the lamppost head-on. The airbag was deployed. Head to toe, he has a scalp laceration above his left eye, bruising and pain to the right shoulder and a query right broken wrist. Patient has admitted that he'd consumed a considerable amount of alcohol and police have done a breath test, which was positive.'

Tom glanced through the notes, keeping his face unreadable. This man had been drinking, another idiot who thought he could get behind the wheel of his car and drive? What would it take before these people realised how much they were endangering others as well as themselves?

'Was anyone else hurt at the scene?'

The paramedic shook his head. 'No. But he came close. Those kids were lucky their mother saw him coming and got them out of the way.'

Kids?

An anger began to simmer within him. He gave a quick nod of thanks to the ambulance team as they took their equipment and left.

His team were already working. Naomi was getting venous access, whilst another doctor was doing a fast scan of the patient's abdomen and another was taking blood-pressure readings.

The X-ray technicians arrived and took pictures of the man's chest and pelvis and Tom ordered pain medication whilst they waited for the results.

Derek had been lucky. Nothing was broken. His wrist was most probably sprained. The only attention he needed was to his scalp, where there was a wound that was deep enough to need stitches, not glue.

Naomi fetched Tom a suturing kit and some sterile gloves and set up a small station on a metal trolley, so that he could work. But first, she cleaned the patient's wound and irrigated it. There was still some airbag dust in and around the wound. At this moment in time, they had no idea how old the patient's car was. If it was an older vehicle, the dust would contain sodium azide, which they definitely didn't want to be embedded in a wound. It was better to be safe, rather than sorry.

'Is that okay?' Naomi asked Derek, noticing he was wincing slightly as she worked.

'It hurts. Can't I get some anaesthetic?'

'Dr Williams will do that for you.'

'How long's that going to take?'

'Do you need to be somewhere?'

'My brother's getting married.'

She put aside the used swabs and grabbed a fresh one to dry the patient's face and around his ear. 'What time?'

'Three o clock.'

'You've plenty of time.'

Tom washed his hands in the sink. It was his job, but dealing with people like Derek still angered him. He'd recklessly endangered others and Tom couldn't help but think that someone like this man had been responsible for killing the love of his life. Derek had been lucky today in more ways than one. He'd had a crash and avoided major injury to himself, but more importantly he hadn't hurt anyone else. Although it sounded like it had been close. It seemed that it was only down to a mother's due diligence that the children had not been hurt.

Would Derek be grumbling about time issues if he'd killed a child?

Tom wiped his hands dry on a paper towel and then turned to pick up the sterile gloves and put them on.

'Hey, Doc, give me the good stuff, yeah? I'm not good with pain.'

Tom wondered who was. He reckoned the physical pain this man was experiencing now was nothing compared to the kind of pain that Tom had gone through. He made no reply but picked up the vial of anaesthetic so he could draw it into the syringe.

He was aware that Naomi was frowning, watching him, confused by his silence, but he had no time to explain it all at this moment. And there was no way in hell he was going to explain it in front of this idiot!

Once he'd got the measurement right, he leaned over the patient to examine the now-cleaned wound and find the best place to insert the anaesthetic. 'This will sting,' he said, finding a tiny modicum of satisfaction when Derek winced and flinched.

'Whoa, Doc!'

He inserted the needle again in another spot and then another, before removing his gloves and going back to the sink to wash his hands. 'That will take a moment.' He looked at Naomi. 'I'll just add the meds to his notes.'

She followed him over to his desk. 'Are you okay? You seem…distracted. Is the gossip still bothering you?'

He looked at her askance. He hadn't given the gossip a moment's notice. 'No.'

'It's just that you don't seem…happy.'

'Well, why would I be?' He marched back over to the patient and washed his hands in the sink once again before putting on another pair of gloves. He didn't notice the odd look Naomi gave him before she left. All he could think about was how to keep his cool whilst dealing with this patient.

Naomi found Jackie in the sluice room, emptying a bedpan.

'Hey, Naomi. What's up?' Jackie was in her usual good mood today.

'Nothing.'

Jackie closed the lid to the machine that disposed of the cardboard pans and pressed the button to activate the mulcher. 'Tell your Aunty Jackie. Come on!'

Naomi shrugged and fiddled with the boxes of gloves

on the shelf beside her. 'Dr Williams is acting odd. More so than usual.'

'Lovers' tiff?' Jackie cackled at her own joke but, seeing her friend's reaction to it, stopped abruptly. 'Oh, yeah, that's right. You two are all "above board".' She wiggled her fingers to make quotation marks in the air.

'We *are*. Flatmates plain and simple.'

'It could be that latest case? The drunk driver?'

'Why would that bother him? We work in A&E; we see drunks all the time.'

Jackie shook her head. 'We do, that's true, but...well, you'd really need to ask him.'

'But I suppose everyone else knows about it?'

'Pretty much. I would have thought you'd know, you've lived with him for a month! Why don't you ask him? If you dare. He's been a lot more prickly lately. I'm not sure I'd want to poke that wasp hive.'

Naomi sank back against the racks. 'You're telling me.'

'I think you'd get away with it.'

She frowned. 'Why?'

Jackie washed her hands, then dried them. 'Because I've seen the way he looks at you.'

That evening, Tom gave her a lift home. He didn't say much in the car and she sensed he had a lot on his mind. Least of all the fact that he had a lodger that he'd never wanted in the first place.

But when they got to the flat and they both had changed, she watched as Tom came out of his room and went over to the piano, looking pensive. His fingertips touched the top of the sleek black instrument and he let them drift across the surface.

Was he thinking about his wife? He'd told Naomi he had

only ever played it for her. Was that case with the drunk driver today somehow connected? And if so, how?

She opened the fridge, looking for inspiration for their evening meal, but there was hardly anything in there. 'I think we need to go to the supermarket.'

Tom looked over to where she stood in the kitchen. 'I'm not sure I feel like that tonight.'

'I don't mind going. Tell me what you'd like and I'll fetch it,' she offered.

He stuck his hands in his pockets and came over to her. 'Do you like seafood?'

'Love it. Why?'

'Then I know a perfect little place.'

The Phoenix was a floating restaurant on the River Thames. It consisted of a beautiful wide yacht with a white hull, a phoenix rising from the ashes painted on the aft.

Naomi hadn't really known what to expect. Certainly, when Tom had suggested that he knew a restaurant they could go to, she'd expected somewhere on dry land. She hadn't known these sorts of things existed, and had had no idea how she ought to dress. In the end, she'd settled on a summery dress, mainly white but with small pink tea roses on it, and then a white shawl for her to wrap around her shoulders.

Tom had given her a nod of approval when she'd emerged from her room and she'd noted his dashing choice of simple black trousers and a tailored white shirt. He looked very handsome, so much so that her stomach had begun to flip and twirl with nervousness and her heart rate had gone up a few notches. She'd hoped she wasn't getting those ugly red blotches on her neck and chest, which was what usually happened when she got nervous, but if she had looked flushed, he didn't mention it.

He'd called a taxi to take them to the restaurant and when they arrived, she'd gasped in awe and surprise at the beautiful fairy lights that lit up the boat and along the gangplank.

Now, she felt Tom's hand at the small of her back as he guided her safely on board.

'Table for two. Williams.'

The maître d' checked his guest list, then escorted them to a table up on the top deck, under a canopy. Across the water, Naomi could see the Houses of Parliament all lit up and the London Eye and although there was a small chill in the air, she didn't feel it. All she felt was excitement.

She had never been somewhere like this. She had never been on a date like this! When she'd met Vincent, it had been in the hospital and she'd known from the beginning what she would be getting into. The only dates she and Vincent had been on were hospital appointments and the occasional drive to a local pub with disabled access. Certainly nothing like this!

She settled into her seat as they were handed the menu. There was a huge selection of seafood dishes: sea bass with lemon capers, a spicy salmon tikka, chilli prawns or a simpler, steamed fish served with vegetables. She decided to go for the prawn starter, the seafood kebab for her main and strawberry cheesecake for dessert.

'Excellent choice,' Tom said, before turning to the waiter. 'I'll have the same.'

The waiter bowed and then disappeared.

Naomi smiled. 'This seems lovely. Thank you for bringing me here.'

'Not at all. You've been cooking so much this week, it's about time you had an evening off.'

'To give the fire alarm a rest, you mean?'

He smiled back and took a sip of his water.

The wine that Tom had ordered, a nice Sauvignon Blanc, arrived. He tested it, giving his approval, and it was poured into both their glasses.

'Have you been here before?' Naomi asked. She wanted to know if he'd been here with his wife. If he had, she didn't think she would mind.

'No. I haven't. It was recommended to me by a colleague.'

'It was a difficult day, today, wasn't it?'

His gaze met hers. 'How do you mean?'

She hesitated, not wanting to spoil the evening right at the start, but also curious to know what had happened in his past. 'On a personal level. That drunk driver.'

Tom sipped his wine and looked out over the water. He seemed to be looking for something. After a moment or two, his gaze returned to her. 'I guess people at work have told you what happened to Meredith?'

She shook her head. 'No. They haven't.'

He seemed surprised, but before he could say any more their chilli prawns arrived. He thanked the waiter and, when he'd gone, he looked back into Naomi's eyes. 'She was killed. By a drunk driver.'

'Oh, no, I'm so sorry, Tom.' She reached out and laid her hand on his. This was the type of person she was. She touched people. She let them know that she understood. His hand under hers felt warm and she wrapped her fingers around his palm. 'If you'd rather I changed the subject...?'

He didn't pull his hand away. But she did see the way he stared down at their hands upon the table. He looked pained. 'It's fine.'

'Tell me about her. I'd like to know who she was.'

His lined brow grew less furrowed and a small light came into his eyes. 'We met at the hospital and she dazzled me from day one. She was this bright, breezy individual, a fantastic nurse, and we just hit it off. I'd rib her about how she'd eat junk food for breakfast on her way into work and she'd joke with me about being a health fanatic just because I'd eaten a banana or something.'

Naomi smiled.

'She called me the health freak, but she was the one who went jogging every day, no matter what the weather.'

'She sounds dedicated.'

'She was. She was jogging on the day she died. She used to wear headphones and listen to music. The driver mounted the kerb and hit her. She wouldn't have heard a thing. Or even have felt it. Or so the paramedics said.'

'I'm so sorry.' She truly meant it. She gave his hand another squeeze and he squeezed back, looking distant for a moment, then he smiled.

'Better eat your prawns, before they get cold.'

The prawns were beautiful. They were buttery and spicy, fat and plump with a hint of garlic and paprika. The freshly baked crusty bread was perfect to help mop up the juices and, when they'd finished, the waiter brought over some finger bowls so they could rinse their fingers.

'That was delicious, thank you,' she told the waiter, who smiled as he cleared their plates.

London at night, on the river, looked beautiful. Naomi had done all the essential touristy things when she'd first arrived, but that had been during the day. Going for a ride on the London Eye had been a treat and she'd looked out over the new city in which she would be living in awe. People came for miles to see this, to experience this. Now here she was seeing it all in a new light and with a great friend by her side.

Because Tom was her friend. She felt they had reached that point now. He was her boss too of course and her landlord, technically, but over time they'd grown quite close.

They'd been working together, living together, sharing meals, sharing a bathroom. She felt she understood him a bit better.

She remembered how when they'd first met, he'd been very standoffish. He'd been prickly and not friendly at all, but then he'd taken her in, making a grand gesture that she truly appreciated. She'd also watched him at work and seen him as the professional, caring, hardworking doctor. And at home he'd become her friend and her cooking instructor! In what seemed like very little time, she'd learnt so much from him in so many ways and now they were here, on this wonderful boat, and she wondered briefly if it was representative of their changing relationship.

She raised her glass for a toast. 'To Meredith.'

Surprise crossed Tom's face and then his expression changed to one of appreciation. He raised his glass and clinked it gently against hers. 'And to new friends.'

'New friends.' She sipped her wine, feeling the gentle fruity flavours wash away the heat of the spicy prawns. This was nice. She was enjoying being here with him. This side of Tom was much, much better than the first side that she'd seen.

The waiter arrived with their main course, which was seafood skewers of monkfish, scallop and salmon, drizzled in a cauliflower sauce, served with buttered carrots and broccoli florets.

They tucked in with gusto, relishing the way the sauce truly brought out the flavours of the fish, until all too soon both their plates were empty. Naomi laughed. 'Is this a sign that my cooking hasn't been as great as I've thought? Have you been secretly starving, Tom?'

He smiled back at her. 'Your food has been delicious.'

'Even the blackened bits?'

'Even those. I think these celebrity chefs are missing

a trick there. Carbonisation of food adds a certain *je ne sais quoi.*'

'Now I know you're lying!'

Tom laughed. 'Living with you has been an eye-opening experience.'

'Why, thank you!' She met his gaze and held it, seeing his eyes sparkling with amusement. 'So has living with you.'

'Oh?'

'I would never have pegged you for a cook.'

'Really? Why not?'

'You seem...' She tried to find the right words. 'You seem the kind of guy who would eat out every night. Restaurants, dinner parties, that sort of thing. Whereas I'm a microwave-meal-for-one kind of girl.'

Tom refilled their wine glasses. 'You mean you're a homebody?'

She nodded. 'Yes, I am. And I like being that. This is great, too, don't get me wrong, but I think there's a lot to be said for staying at home in your pyjamas and eating a bowl of popcorn in front of the television.'

'You're absolutely right. Homes are underrated.'

She looked at him. 'And your home? Do you enjoy being there?'

He pursed his lips momentarily and the action drew her focus. He had such a lovely mouth. A wide smile, good teeth. He didn't smile often enough, but when he did... It couldn't fail to make anyone smile with him. 'I do now.'

She swallowed. Did he mean that he enjoyed being there now that *she* was there? Perhaps she was no longer the interloper. No longer the unwanted tenant. 'Really?'

'Really. I think I'll miss you, when you leave.'

'It'll be quieter, you mean?' she suggested.

'It'll be...emptier.'

She sipped her wine and wondered what he meant by that.

The cheesecake arrived and, on a par with the previous courses, it was absolutely delicious, just as she'd expected. By the time they'd finished eating, Naomi was feeling comfortably full so they had coffee and then Tom suggested a walk along the river.

Naomi wrapped her shawl around her shoulders, glad that she'd brought it. It was a warm evening for early March but the air was slowly getting colder and her shawl wasn't enough. Tom proffered his jacket, wrapping it around her shoulders, and she snuggled into its warm depths. 'Thank you.'

'No problem.'

She smiled and looked up at him. Suddenly, it occurred to her that he seemed so alone. Not lonely. *Alone*. A man whose only companion was a grief that he'd carried with him for a long time. She wished she could make it better for him.

'You know…when I lost Vincent, it was expected. We'd known for months that the end was coming and we both hoped that it would be easier. You know? That we'd have had our chance to say goodbye to each other. Do you find that difficult, Tom? That you never had the opportunity or time to say goodbye? Is that why it still hurts you so much?'

He shrugged. 'Maybe. We'd had so little time together. I think it hurts because…well, because I'd had all these dreams for us—travelling, children—and that future has been taken away.'

She could understand. Her hopes and dreams for a future had been taken from her, too. 'Perhaps we've both got different futures awaiting us. And they may be different from the ones we were expecting, but perhaps they won't be as bad as we expect.'

He gave a grim laugh. 'For you, maybe. I'm not planning on getting involved with anyone again, remember? You still believe that there's another soulmate out there for you, so your future still shines bright with possibility.'

A couple walked towards them, looking so in love, so comfortable with each other. They had their arms around each other, the woman leaning her head against her partner's shoulder as he kissed the top of her hair. Naomi smiled at them as they walked past.

'I think there's someone out there for you, Tom. You've just got to look harder.'

She could feel his gaze upon her and she glanced up at him and smiled. She stopped walking for a moment and when he stilled and faced her, she tentatively reached for his hand and grasped it in her own. 'Promise me, Tom, that you'll look for her.'

'I—'

'I don't think you should be alone. Not for the rest of your life. That's a long time to be blind to the possibilities all around you.'

'You're very kind, Naomi.' He pushed back a loose strand of her hair, tucking it behind her ear. His eyes sparkled in the moonlight. Standing here, holding his hand by the riverside, seemed the right thing to be doing. Their relationship had changed so much and, where once she had been apprehensive around him, she now felt that she cared. That she wanted good things for him, and the idea that he would be alone for the rest of his life...

He was staring down at her, intently.

They were both standing so close to the other that she suddenly became aware of the small space between them, almost as if it were crackling with unseen electricity.

His eyes stared deep into her soul, and it was as if she

could feel him searching, see him looking for something within her that only he could find. And he took a step closer.

Naomi sucked in her breath, her lips parting as he came closer. Did she want Tom to kiss her?

Yes. Absolutely.

Suddenly the realisation of how much she wanted to kiss him slammed through her, making its presence felt. It felt as if this, the kiss that was about to happen, was the most obvious thing in the world. As if it were something she had always wanted and wondered about, only she hadn't allowed herself to think about it, or acknowledge it. Yet here it was and…

It was like everything was happening in slow motion.

Tom was moving closer. His head lowered to hers, their eyes closing as his lips approached hers.

Naomi held her breath, awaiting the touch of his lips, her heart pounding, her breathing fast and shallow. Could he hear her heart? Did he know how much she suddenly wanted this?

But where was the kiss?

She felt his hand pull free of hers and she opened her eyes to see him stand up straight again, wearing an agonised expression of pain and regret. 'I'm sorry…I can't…'

It was horrible. She wished she could give him what he needed and ease his pain. Make him feel that there was still a chance of happiness for him.

He began to walk again, waiting for her to follow alongside. 'I'm sorry, Naomi.'

'It doesn't matter,' she said, trying to make him feel better, but inside she felt crushed. She was bitterly disappointed.

It does matter!

Could she really have *kissed* Tom? She risked a quick glance at him. Yes, he was gorgeous and yes, she liked him.

In fact, she liked him a lot, but would kissing him really be wise? Perhaps it was a good thing that he'd paused and thought better of it.

He was her boss, her friend and her flatmate. Kissing him would have simply opened up a whole world of complication that she didn't need! When she thought about it sensibly, she knew it was probably a bad idea. After all, the man was obviously still in a quagmire of grief, wasn't he?

He was a man of deep feeling. She knew that. She saw proof of it on a daily basis. Now she had no doubt that if they were to kiss, then Tom would make her feel things that she had never felt before. Vincent, for all his sweetness and vulnerability, had never been an overtly passionate kisser. Their kisses had always been friendly. They had mostly been kisses of greeting, hello and goodbye. Vanilla kisses. Their whole relationship had been about being safe. About being careful and controlled. That was the reason why he'd been such a great husband, and one who she missed dearly.

But had she ever yearned for him? Had she ever been desperate for Vincent's touch?

No. That wasn't what their relationship had been based on.

So now? Being here with Tom, feeling the sudden desire to know what his kisses would be like, and where they might lead...

It was terrifying!

But it was also exciting. And a little bit dangerous. She could feel adrenaline zipping through her system like electrical shocks. She felt as if she could run. She felt as if she could achieve anything if she dared.

Except kiss him.

Just because she wanted to do it, it didn't make it right. Surely this was her worst nightmare. Getting involved with a handsome man, as she'd seen her mother do so many times, only to be used and cast aside later. Because wasn't that what they all did? Wasn't that what she had learned? The one thing she had decided upon from a young age was to never get involved with someone that dangerous.

And Tom was the worst kind of dangerous.

He wasn't free to be loved.

CHAPTER SIX

SHE'D SPENT MOST of last night lying in her bed thinking about the almost-kiss, and sleep had eluded her for a while. She'd expected to wake up feeling tired and awful, but to her surprise she didn't. Her new mindset had given her the energy and determination to make everything right again.

She'd decided as he'd driven her to work that she wouldn't mention it. Tom obviously regretted the moment and she didn't want him to feel embarrassed or awkward around her. Nor did she want to feel awkward around him. She wanted them to go back to the way they'd been before the almost-kiss. Good friends. Good flatmates. Boss and employee. Team players.

If she saw Tom today at the hospital, she would wish him good morning, smile and then get on with her day. If he raised the issue with her, then that would be different. But still, she'd listen and nod and smile and tell him it was all fine. She'd decided that she wouldn't put any pressure on him whatsoever. She would be strong and independent. She would not be clingy, or whiny or make him feel as if he'd almost kissed the wrong woman. She didn't want him to think she was someone who might turn into a weird stalker, desperate for his affections.

She put her coat into her locker, changed into her uniform and twisted her hair up into a clip. Then she headed to the staffroom to make herself a quick cup of coffee. She made drinks for Jackie, Stefan and Bobby too and settled down with her notepad and pen, waiting for the sister from the night shift to come in and do the handover.

Dr Thomas walked in, followed by a couple of health-care assistants, then another doctor.

She wondered where Tom was.

It doesn't matter, she told herself. *Be bright and breezy.*

And then…in he came. He was looking tall and delicious as always and his gaze found hers in an instant, before he quickly looked away.

Her smile froze on her face.

It was easy to tell yourself that you wouldn't let it matter. It was easy to *say* that you wouldn't show a reaction. But reality was just a little tougher and *doing* it was another matter entirely. Having him here so close to her made her entire body feel as if it were revving its engine, as if someone had pressed down on the accelerator, making the engine roar. She could feel her blood thrumming through her veins and could feel herself beginning to overheat.

It had been the same that morning, when Tom had driven her in to work. He'd barely said a word, but she'd been so aware of him next to her, just inches away. Every time he'd reached for the gear stick to change up or down, she'd sucked in a breath.

She didn't know why this was happening. She hadn't felt this way before he'd tried to kiss her. But now, after that moment, something had changed.

She dipped her head and sipped her coffee, aware of his every step, his every movement. He was making himself a drink and, although she wanted to watch him whilst his back was turned and try to gauge his mood or how he might feel about her, she kept staring straight ahead. He would be a perfect gentleman, of that she had no doubt.

Jackie said something to her and Naomi made a sound as if in agreement, but really she had no idea what her friend had just said.

She sipped her coffee again and stared at her notepad on the desk in front of her.

Just look at the notepad. Look at that and nothing else. Tom is just another person in the room. Don't look at him.

She looked at him. She took in the broad expanse of his back, the neatness of his small, trim waist. The way his hair neatly met the collar of his shirt, the soft curve of muscle beneath the material.

He'd tried to kiss her. He'd tried and so it *did* mean something! Because surely there had to be feelings behind that intention. Surely he must have felt an attraction to her.

She averted her gaze as he turned round to find a seat, intently aware of him moving round to sit next to Dr Thomas, out of her eyeline.

Thank you. At least now I'll be able to concentrate.

She took another sip of her coffee, willing herself to concentrate on something else.

Naomi was assigned to work in Minors. As was Tom. No matter, she thought. It didn't mean they were necessarily going to run into each other all day. It was a big enough department, with sixteen cubicles. As long as she kept busy, it should be fine. And A&E was *always* busy.

She had no patient already assigned to her, so she went to pick up the next patient card from triage.

Logan Reed, aged twenty, who had a cut on his leg.

She called him through, noting that he was a tall, young man, quite lanky in appearance, a little pale and weak-looking. She led him through to her cubicle and asked him to sit on the bed.

'So, Logan, what's brought you to A&E today?'

He answered her in a dull voice. 'I've cut my leg.'

'And how did you do that?'

He shrugged.

She sensed there was more to this, something he was afraid to say. 'Can you show me whereabouts on your leg the cut is?'

He stood up and unzipped his trousers, lowering them to his knees. He didn't look at her or make eye contact, but just waited whilst she took in the multitude of scars across the tops of his thighs. On one thigh there was a section covered with a gauze pad.

It was now clear Logan had been self-harming and her heart sank. What could be causing this boy so much pain that he felt he had to do this?

'Okay. Do you want to lie back for me? Then I'll have a look at this cut.'

He positioned himself on the bed and waited.

Naomi put on some gloves and removed the gauze pad. Whilst he'd obviously cut himself again, this gash was bigger than the others and quite possibly deeper. It was still bleeding, but it looked as if it had slowed.

'What did you use?' she asked, trying to keep her voice calm.

Logan shrugged. 'A craft blade.'

'Was it clean?'

He nodded.

She delicately replaced the gauze pad and removed her gloves. 'And what made you do this? Today? What happened to make you cut yourself worse than all the other times?'

His gaze met hers, briefly. 'A girl. You probably think I'm stupid.'

Naomi didn't. She knew people dealt with their pain in many different ways. Some just cried, whilst others buried themselves in work so that they didn't have to think.

Some people would exercise furiously and others would just wallow deep in depression. Then others, like Logan, self-harmed, perhaps preferring to feel physical pain, rather than the emotional one.

'No! No, I don't. Were you in a relationship with this girl?'

'I thought I was. I thought we were serious. Turns out she was just having fun.' He sounded bitter. She could understand his hurt.

'This might need stitches, Logan. I'll need to get a doctor to assess it properly in order to do that.'

'I know the drill. If it does need stitches, will I get an anaesthetic?'

Naomi thought that was an odd question. 'Of course you will. Why?'

'Last time I needed stitches I went to a hospital—not this one—and they said that if I could cut myself without anaesthetic, I could get stitched up without it, too.'

Naomi was horrified. 'What? That's awful!'

'In some places, when you self-harm, they treat you like you deserve it.'

'Well, we don't do that here! There are protocols in place. You won't be treated differently from anyone else.'

Logan nodded approvingly. 'Glad to hear it.'

'Are you receiving treatment for your self-harming, Logan? Are you seeing anyone?'

'I was. But I haven't for a while.'

'Then I'll refer you for another assessment. Is that all right?'

'Sure.'

She nodded. 'Are you in pain? From the cut?'

'A bit, but it's okay.'

'No. It's not okay. It's never okay to be in pain.'

She went in search of an available doctor, hoping to

maybe find Dr Thomas, or one of the others on duty. But they were already busy. The one doctor that had just finished with a patient and was about to see another was Tom.

Naomi relaxed her shoulders, letting out a low, long breath, and then she went over to him. She kept her manner businesslike. The epitome of professionalism. 'Tom, could I ask you to check my patient over, if you're free?'

He met her gaze and nodded. 'Of course. Who's the patient?'

'Logan Reed. He's self-harmed, and cut his leg. It needs an assessment and possibly stitches.'

'Has he got a current mental-health referral?'

'No, but he's had counselling before. I think he's fallen off the wagon somewhat, so I'm going to re-refer him.'

'Okay, let me take a look.'

They walked side by side to the cubicle, neither looking at the other, but each totally aware of how close they stood.

Naomi pulled open the cubicle curtain and introduced Logan to Tom, who put on some gloves and examined the wound. 'Can you feel me touching here? And here?' he asked Logan.

The young man nodded. 'Yes.'

'You can wiggle your toes and move your leg with no problems?'

'It's fine.'

'Good. I don't think it's too deep. It needs a clean and then I can stitch it. It's probably going to need at least three stitches. They'll be dissolvable, so there's no need to go to the doctor's to get them removed.'

Logan nodded again.

'What made you do this?' Tom asked, quietly.

Their patient let out a long sigh. 'This girl I was into. She was beautiful, you know? Popular. All the guys wanted to be with her and she picked me. I thought we had something special. This deep connection. But it turned out, she wasn't as into me as I was her.'

Naomi tried her hardest not to look at Tom's face. She'd thought Tom had sensed something between them, too. But she couldn't imagine what this poor young boy was feeling. To only be twenty years old, but to have more scars than years on his legs. She wondered what had gone wrong in his life, which compelled him to do such a thing in order to cope with emotional pain.

She thought of her own pain. The hurt and the grief she'd felt at the loss of her marriage. She'd dreamt of being married ever since she'd been a little girl. Her mother had raised her to believe that she could not be complete without a man, and that finding love was the ultimate goal. So as a child, she'd idolised marriage as the epitome of love. The way you would show the world how dedicated you were to another person. She'd drawn pictures of her ideal dress, imagined her perfect wedding day, dreamed about her perfect groom and how her life would be as a married woman.

But she'd had none of that. Meeting Vincent had changed it all. Suddenly she'd found a way to be married without leaving herself at risk of having that man walk out on her or cheat on her. She and Vincent might not have been able to have a physical relationship, but she'd told herself that didn't matter so much. So long as she was safe. And her heart was protected. She'd known that Vincent would die young and she would lose him quickly, but she'd felt that that was something she would deal with when the time came. She would still be able to tell the world, tell herself, that she had been married, had been in love and that she'd had a *good* marriage. That she'd not been desperate and unloved like her own mother, who had seemed like the loneliest woman on the planet.

Eight years she'd spent with Vincent. Eight years of being best friends with her husband: sharing the same jokes, sharing quiet times—reading books, having picnics, taking day trips to the beach or a country house. Eight years of doing the things couples did together. Of caring for him. Loving him.

Eight years of repressing her excitement, her joy, her passion for life.

We all deal with pain and suffering in different ways.

Her own suffering had turned her into a stronger woman. She felt sure of that. Now, she was single and strong and determined. She was free to live her life the way she wanted, without anything holding her back. She could have let her pain control her. She could have let her grief override her emotions, but she hadn't.

And look at Tom. He'd lost his wife. His suffering could have turned him into a bitter individual, angry at the world. But he was kind and considerate and friendly. What was it that made one person strong and determined not to be bowed down by tragedy, whilst others could barely cope?

Although, she knew better than anyone that sometimes grief and pain could still affect you, even when you thought you were over it. Tom had held back yesterday, for example. She'd seen the pain in his eyes, and it seemed Tom was still not over his wife's death. Maybe he still felt married. After all, he'd not chosen to end his marriage. His wife had been taken from him. Did he still have feelings for Meredith? Had he bowed his head to kiss Naomi and suddenly realised what he was doing?

Of course. Tom still loved his dead wife. He clearly felt like he had betrayed Meredith, by attempting to kiss Naomi.

If that were true, then it was definitely a good thing that he'd put the brakes on. He obviously wasn't in the right head space for her to get involved with him. She didn't want to be involved with a man who wasn't free. She didn't want to be involved with a man who still loved another woman.

She stood there, cleaning Logan's wound with saline, trying to be delicate, trying not to hurt him, until Tom could administer the anaesthetic.

All the while, she promised herself that from now on she would start looking harder for a flat. A place of her own. Tom clearly needed his space back. His life back.

The atmosphere between them needed lightening up. But how could she do that? Perhaps she should suggest they do something fun. Something that neither of them had ever done. Something that would get them both out of the flat, both out of that space where Tom's grim memories resided and back out into the world. Most of all, something that had nothing to do with relationships and kisses and heightened moments of tension.

They could still be friends. Good friends, even. But for her, flat-hunting was going to be a number-one priority from now on.

Tom was off-limits.

And so was she.

Tom watched Logan limp out of the department and went to write up the patient notes. He'd left Naomi clearing up the cubicle and suddenly felt a lot more relaxed than when he had been encased with her inside that small space.

His discomfort with her proximity hadn't stopped them from treating Logan to the best of their abilities. But he hoped and prayed that this current level of unease would soon pass. The last thing he wanted was for work to feel uncomfortable, just because of what had happened with Naomi.

He knew he had to forget the moment, but it was difficult. He'd loved Meredith. Of course he had. Their relationship had been built not just on love but friendship, too. But what about Naomi? That *need* to kiss her had just popped up out of nowhere, completely unexpected. He hadn't thought, *Well, this is a nice moonlit walk by the river, that's romantic, I'll kiss her.* It had just happened. They'd stood there, looking at each other, and suddenly Tom had just…*needed* her.

It had just seemed right. He'd felt comfortable with her. They'd been having a pleasant walk, enjoying a good conversation and she'd been so lovely, so beautiful, listening to everything he'd said, paying attention. She'd been funny and humble and such good company and he'd not been able to remember the last time he'd felt that good. Then he'd just felt the need to…

He sighed.

He'd almost kissed her and then had walked away without a word of explanation. She must have been angry with him and she must have had questions. And yet she hadn't asked him about it. She hadn't pressured him into talking. She was even being sweet today, her normal and professional self. There had been no unfriendly atmosphere between them, as he'd feared, especially after the drive that morning when she hadn't said a word. He'd been silent, too, waiting for her to say something. To receive a verbal assault, *anything*, but she'd remained calm and serene. And he truly appreciated that.

Maybe he was wrong. Maybe it hadn't meant as much to her as it had to him.

Tom looked up and saw Naomi walking towards him. Suddenly, he knew he had to apologise. Or at least he had to say something.

'Tom, can we talk?'

There were other members of staff milling around. Stefan was writing on a blood sample and Jackie was nearby, washing her hands in the sink.

'Of course. But it'll have to be at break.'

'I have a break at ten-thirty. Will you come and find me?'

He nodded. He watched her pick up another patient card and disappear to the waiting room.

Even after the way he'd treated her, she still acted with dignity, as if nothing had happened. He couldn't be more grateful.

When it got to ten-thirty, he found her dismissing her last patient. They both made a drink in the staffroom and sat opposite each other over the long table.

Naomi gave him a brief, polite smile, before she opened her mouth to speak. 'I've decided that what we both need is an evening of fun.'

Tom blinked. This wasn't what he'd been expecting. 'Okay.'

'We've both been through an awful lot of stress in our personal lives and everything has just been so intense. We need to break free of that and do something random and fun, to forget work and life's stresses and just enjoy *being*. What do you think?'

He gave a simple nod. 'I agree.' He liked the idea. She was right. 'Absolutely.' A smile crept across his face as he realised just how much he was beginning to really like this woman.

'Good. I've arranged something I've never done before and hopefully something you haven't done either. We'll have a laugh and enjoy ourselves and just let everything go. Okay?'

Tom nodded. 'Are you going to tell me what it is?'

She smiled at him. 'No. Not until we get there.'

'Right.'

She stood up. 'Right. I'll see you later.'

As she walked away he shook his head in disbelief. What had he done so right in his life that Naomi had been allowed to walk into it?

Then he laughed quietly to himself. He hadn't thought that when he'd first met her. He'd thought she was a clumsy rule-breaker, who had demanded his attention.

But now?

She was brightening up his life.

'We're doing *what*?' Tom looked at her as if she'd just suggested they go parachuting naked.

'A roller disco derby.'

'On skates?'

'Roller skates, yes. Don't worry, Tom. They give you helmets and everything.'

'But…*you*, on skates. Is that safe?'

She gave him a playful nudge and laughed. 'I'll stay upright and everything. Come on, it'll be fun. Eighties music, a bit of disco lighting and a whole room full of adults who all ought to know better. What could be more right?' She took hold of his hand and he allowed himself to be pulled forward, a grin on his face.

The large wooden-floored skating arena was filled with flashing disco lights and the heavy beat of loud bass-heavy music. Tom could almost feel the beat thrumming through his bones. Skaters—who'd obviously done this before—whizzed past him, whilst other people stumbled along carefully, as he was doing.

Naomi held his hand in hers and, laughing, pulled him onto the wooden floor.

'Hang on! Just let me grab this.' He reached for the side,

smiling broadly as his hand gripped the safety rail and he could suddenly stand fully upright once again.

Naomi stood by him smiling. 'We'll do this together!' she shouted. 'One step at a time, yes?'

He nodded and wondered what everyone at work would say if they could see him now. At the rate he was going, they might well see him, when he went to A&E later as a *patient* rather than a doctor, with a sprained ankle. But with a faltering lunge, he let go of the side and allowed Naomi to lead him.

The battle for his balance was an awkward one. He imagined he must look like a baby deer on stilts, all long legs and awkward wobbles, but Naomi was wobbling all over the place, too, so he didn't feel like a total idiot. There were lots of people struggling, but everyone was laughing and those that did fall down were soon picked up by those around them.

When had he *ever* had so much carefree fun?

He would never have thought to come and do this on his own. Nor would he have let any of his other colleagues even suggest it! But Naomi had managed to get him here, had managed to put wheels on his feet and make him move.

Another skater whizzed past quickly, sending Tom's arms whirling, and suddenly his feet had been lost from under him and he smacked down hard on his rump.

Naomi was bent double with laughter, but she shuffled over to give him a hand up. He was laughing so hard his sides were beginning to hurt. When he was at last back up on his 'feet' he clutched her hand and mouthed a 'thank you' as they began to skate again.

He had no idea how long they were on the arena floor, but pretty soon he started to get the hang of it and began to pick up speed. Naomi continued to stumble around behind him, so he doubled back and this time grabbed her hand.

'Come on!' he encouraged her, helping her to keep up with him.

Who would have thought it? Dr Tom Williams skating, and actually enjoying himself, at a roller derby! Happily, he surged forward, but then all of a sudden he felt Naomi start to wobble and he turned to catch her, doing it without thinking.

Suddenly she was in his arms again. Up close, he could see the sparkle in her eyes and he couldn't look away. She was *so* beautiful! And she felt so right in his embrace. Her smile faltered briefly as she saw him gaze at her mouth, but then it returned and Tom knew that *this time*, he *had* to kiss her.

Slowly, in the middle of the roller derby, with everyone dashing past with lights flashing and the music pounding, the rest of the world faded away. For just a moment, it was only the two of them, wrapped in a world of magic and wonder. He dipped his head and let his lips touch hers.

He closed his eyes.

Her lips were so soft, so warm. Her arms came up around his neck and he pulled her closer against him. She felt so good. So right.

He allowed himself to be lost in the kiss. To just enjoy it. He would worry about the consequences later. Right now, in this moment, it was just Naomi and him.

The kiss deepened and grew more intense. He felt hungry for her; he desired her, wanted her. How was it possible that he could lose himself so easily? So readily?

But he pushed that thought away.

Someone caught his arm as they raced past and it broke the intensity of the moment.

She stared back at him as they parted, surprise and desire in her eyes, and he moistened his lips, before smiling uncertainly and taking her hand once again. They began to skate, but now it felt different.

The kiss had changed everything between them. The dynamics, the atmosphere…

And then it came.

The guilt. The pain. The flood of past memories, images of Meredith in the sunshine, laughing at him, calling his name, reaching out to him.

But his hand was in Naomi's. And he couldn't let go.

He needed a break. A minute to breathe.

He headed over to the safety rail.

The next week passed in a blur. Tom threw himself into his work once again, determined to get through every patient. He took blood samples, he stitched cuts, he sent patients to X-ray or CT. He was curt with everyone, no longer bothering to stop and chat, grabbing coffee on the go and not taking his full break.

He saw Naomi everywhere, it seemed. She was in the sluice, the drugs cupboard, holding patients' hands, tucking them in or helping them to walk, helping them to deal with whatever health issue had brought them to A&E. He tried his best to ignore her. He kept his head down and walked past, keeping their interactions to a minimum.

But it was difficult. It pained him to do it. It was completely out of his character to treat a colleague like this. He knew he was being rude. He noticed the reactions of the other staff when he stormed past. He saw those questioning looks and the furtively raised eyebrows. He'd even heard a few whispering, asking, 'What's got into Tom?'

He *had* changed. He sensed it. He heard it in his voice when he spoke to people, felt it in his demeanour and hated himself whenever he was terse with someone who normally he would be cordial with.

It pained him to think what Naomi must think about his change in demeanour. She had to have noticed. But, of course, she was acting like the consummate professional she was. Always patient. Always kind and considerate. There was always a smile on her face for the patients. She interacted with him as little as was possible, but did so with extreme politeness. For example, there had been that last case, an hour or so ago, the lady with the broken wrist. He'd confirmed the break to the patient and explained that she would need a cast whilst Naomi had just stood there, looking at her patient. When he had finished and had turned to go, she'd addressed him with a simple, 'Thank you, Dr Williams.' Then she'd turned back to her patient.

That was it.

He couldn't stand it. It all seemed so false. For him, there were plenty of emotions still simmering below the surface since the kiss they'd shared, but was it the same for her?

He knew he shouldn't let it bother him. That he needed to forget it. He knew getting involved with Naomi was the wrong thing to do.

Because despite the way he was acting, he wasn't indifferent to Naomi. That was the whole problem. He wasn't indifferent to her at all. And if she was suffering as well, because of him? Well, they both had to be adults enough to sort that out. He was damned if he was going to let it affect them any longer. Especially at work. Neither of them could afford to be distracted or to make any mistakes. Mistakes could cause serious danger to a patient.

He couldn't let that happen.

Naomi sank back against the toilet door, her eyes closed, as tears began to threaten to spill.

What on earth was going on? One minute they'd been

having fun, just letting off steam, trying to stay upright and the next moment she'd been in Tom's arms and things had started to get steamy!

How could a single kiss have such power to disturb two people?

Everything had changed the very second his lips had broken away from hers. She could see it in his eyes, the way his expression changed, as if he'd suddenly closed himself off from her, when all she wanted to do was talk about what had happened.

She needed to talk about that kiss! It had felt…monumental! Lip-tingling, body-scorching, heart-poundingly good! She'd never felt that before. Ever. Was this the type of passion she'd read about in love stories? Was this what it was meant to feel like? Because she had all these weird sensations and feelings whizzing through her system and she didn't know what she was supposed to do with them. Or how she was supposed to react to them. Her body felt alive, out of her control. Whenever she was with him, it was like her body was suddenly on alert, aware, and her heart would pound again, her mouth would go dry, her breathing would quicken. Yet Tom was acting weird and she didn't know what to do.

Did he regret their kiss?

She so badly wanted to ask him about it, but he was staying out of her way, not giving her the opportunity to talk about it. At home he either stayed in his room, or he went out. At work, he'd begun throwing himself into his cases again, acting cold as he'd been when she'd first met him. She felt like she was losing him.

Don't do this to me, Tom.

She needed to understand what was happening. Needed to make sense of it. For her, the kiss had been an experience that she would happily experience again and again.

She'd not known it was possible to feel that good. To feel that alive! And the fact that she'd felt that with Tom...

Tears began to run down her cheeks, but not from the hurt at being ignored. She was crying because she'd felt something so magical, something she'd never believed could have existed, and now it looked as if she would never experience that again.

She needed to talk to Tom.

They *both* needed to sort this out.

Naomi was returning the ECG machine to its proper place when Stefan strolled over to her.

'Hey, Naomi.'

She wished Tom would approach her just as easily. But the one man she wanted to talk to her was still avoiding her like crazy.

'Stefan.'

'I was wondering...have you heard of the Spring Ball? For the staff?'

'Err...I think I've seen the signs up for it on the notice boards, yes.' Naomi noticed Tom emerge from a cubicle and her gaze tracked him as he came over to the desk not far away and sat down, yet again, without making eye contact.

Stefan continued. 'I thought maybe you'd like to go with me? As my date?'

Naomi watched, but Tom continued to write, focused intently on his work. He probably hadn't heard what Stefan just said. He was so fixated on blocking out anything to do with her.

Going to the staff Spring Ball wasn't something she would normally be interested in, but hadn't she promised herself to be independent? She should be enjoying life. She should be trying out all these things she wouldn't normally do, now that she had the freedom to do them.

Letting Stefan take her wasn't what she wanted. She wanted Tom to take her. She wanted to walk in on his arm. To dance with him and enjoy a special night together. But he'd made it very clear that the kiss had been a terrible mistake. That she had been a terrible mistake. And that he wanted nothing to do with her in *that* way.

Well, fine!

She couldn't go to the ball alone and she couldn't see Tom taking her now, so... 'Sure. That'd be nice. Thank you.'

Stefan beamed. 'Great! That's fantastic! There's...something else actually. Jackie mentioned that you were looking for somewhere to live.'

She glanced at Tom, feeling her cheeks flame with heat, hating the way all of this was making her feel. It felt as if she might cry at any moment. She didn't want to move out. Not really. But she'd been forced into a corner by the whole situation and things were so difficult with Tom. It was probably best for her to leave. In fact, he'd likely be pleased to get rid of her. 'That's right.'

'I know of a place that's just come free in my block. I could get you a viewing, if you wanted? It has two bedrooms. Pretty decent. And the rent's not too high.'

'Oh...right. Erm...yes, sure, I'll take a look. Can't stay where I am forever, can I?'

Tom grabbed his notes and strode off, his eyes cold, his face impassive.

It was clear that he'd heard. Inside, Naomi felt devastated, but she wasn't sure what else she could have done. He wasn't even talking to her any more and his rejection of her hurt. She couldn't stay in his flat now. It had only been meant to be a temporary solution in the first place anyway and she'd been there fast approaching six weeks!

She was doing Tom a favour by moving. She was getting out of his hair, out of his life. It was what he was clearly asking for.

It was what he needed.

And if she was going to protect her heart...then it was what she needed, too.

CHAPTER SEVEN

EIGHT HOURS INTO his shift, Tom was standing in the waiting area of A&E watching his last patient hobble away on a new pair of crutches. Once his patient was safely through the double doors and on their way back home, he turned to hand some paperwork to the receptionist, but was suddenly tapped on the shoulder from behind.

'Excuse me, are you a doctor?'

Tom turned to see a tall man like himself, who was probably in his eighties, looking as grey as a ghost and sweating slightly. 'Are you all right, sir?'

'I don't feel very well, no,' the man replied.

His complexion, the sweating and the general look of confusion in the man's eyes told Tom that this was serious. His instinct went into overdrive and he grabbed the nearest wheelchair and manoeuvred the man into it gently. Then he turned around quickly and whisked the man through to Resus.

'What's your name, sir?' he asked as he pushed the man through the department, avoiding obstacles in his path and trying not to show the patient that he was close to a crash in more ways than one.

The patient didn't answer but just gazed about him as they passed through corridors and finally the double doors that led to the heart of A&E.

Tom would need assistance. He needed a nurse, some-one to help him with this patient and his assessment.

He saw Naomi coming out of the locker room, looking as beautiful as always, if a little paler than usual. His heart sank. He'd hoped he wouldn't have to ask her.

But he had to.

Patient care came first over personal issues.

'Naomi? Can you give me a hand?'

He saw the look of shock register on her face, then she resumed her professional air and smiled at the patient, before hurrying along beside them.

He burst through the double doors into Resus and parked the patient in his chair next to an empty bed. Turning to Naomi, he whispered, 'I think this guy's having a heart attack.'

He was too close. It reminded him of that kiss. Of feeling her there in his arms, breathing in her aroma, just *holding* her. And of the delight of her lips upon his. Abruptly—disturbed by the sudden outpouring of this memory—he turned away. 'Sir, can you get on this trolley for me?' There were no other patients in Resus. The department had their cases and all the other patients had been sent up to various wards or back home.

The old man stood on wobbly, weak legs, whilst Tom and Naomi held him steady as he turned to sit on the edge of the trolley.

'I'd better…take off…my shoes…' The man bent forward to remove his shoes and swayed dizzily.

They both grabbed him quickly, pushing him back against the bed and sweeping up the patient's legs. 'Your shoes are fine, sir. Up you go now.'

Tom quickly strode over to the ECG machine and dragged it across the floor. 'Can you remove your shirt for me?'

The man nodded slowly, as if he was hearing the instructions in slow motion. He seemed unable to focus on anything, with his head bobbing about like a boat at sea, as he slowly tried to coordinate his arms to lift off his jumper and shirt underneath.

It was taking too long. If this man was having a cardiac event, as Tom suspected, then losing all these precious seconds could have a fatal effect.

'Here, we'll help you.' He grabbed the hem of the jumper and shirt and pulled them over the man's head in one swift movement, so that Naomi could start attaching the leads to the patient's chest. Thankfully, the man wasn't too hairy, saving them a few more precious seconds that would have been wasted on shaving him to attach the electrodes. 'How long have you been feeling unwell, sir?'

'I don't… Was in the garden…' he mumbled, saying something further that Tom couldn't quite catch.

Naomi was just finishing attaching all the electrodes. She'd worked quickly and expertly, aware of the urgency, but not allowing it to overwhelm her. When she was done, she gave Tom a nod.

'Lie still for a moment, please, sir.'

Tom pressed the button to start the ECG recording the electrical impulses of the patient's heart. Whilst he waited for the trace to begin, Naomi wrapped a blood-pressure cuff around the man's arm and Tom put an oxygen mask over the patient's face and set it to full flow.

'Sir? Have you got any allergies? Anything I should know about?' Tom asked, leaning over the bed, his ear close to the patient's face so that he could hear an answer. Naomi grabbed the handset for the internal phone system and got through to Reception. 'Bleep Dr Thomas to Resus, please,' she instructed.

He glanced at the trace on the ECG machine. There was an acute ST elevation, indicating, along with his patient's other signs of confusion and waxy, pale skin, sure signs of a myocardial infarction.

He needed IV access and blood samples. He worked quickly, his mind buzzing, all his procedures and protocols running through his head like a military parade—in order, logical, precise.

This was what he loved doing. This was what he thrived on. Pressure, adrenaline, precision. Making decisions, reacting, recording, acting appropriately, *saving lives*.

'What's happening?' the patient mumbled through the mask, his head thrashing this way and that.

The double doors were pushed open as Dr Thomas arrived. The second he strode into the room, before the double doors had even swung closed again, the patient stopped moving and let out one long, heavy breath.

Naomi smacked the red emergency buzzer on the wall, calling for more assistance, and reached behind the trolley for the lever that would collapse it down flat.

Tom bent low over the patient, checking for breathing, watching for signs of his rising chest, but there was nothing. His fingers reached for the man's pulse.

Nothing.

In an instant, he stood and brought his fist down on the patient's chest.

Still nothing. The ECG showed ventricular tachycardia.

Tom hurriedly grabbed the defibrillator pads and placed them onto the man's chest, pressing the button and making the machine charge its joules ready for the shock. He looked around the patient's bed, making sure Dr Thomas, Naomi and the rapidly arriving team members were not touching the patient.

'Stand clear! Shocking!' He pressed the button again and the patient jerked slightly on the bed.

Naomi felt for a pulse and found one. 'We've got him back.'

Looks of relief were on the faces of everyone surrounding the bed as the patient slowly came to, blinking, before he promptly tore off the mask and vomited over the side railings.

When he'd recovered and been handed one of the cardboard bowls, the patient wiped his mouth and then looked around him at the mass of people. 'What happened?'

Tom stepped aside, avoiding the mess on the floor, and came to the other side of the patient's bed. 'What do you remember?'

'I was in my garden. I felt...odd. Thought I'd better come to A&E. I can't remember much more than that.'

Tom had seen that before. For some lucky people, the body prevented the mind from remembering something so traumatic and painful as a heart attack.

'You've had a heart attack, sir. What's your name?'

'Edward Stovey.'

'Well, Edward. You've been a very lucky man today.'

'Have I?'

Naomi reached for the man's hand and placed it in hers comfortingly. 'We nearly lost you there.'

Edward sighed. 'Wouldn't have really mattered if you had.'

Tom frowned. 'Of course it would. It would have mattered to us.' Losing any patient was something Tom didn't tolerate very well. To him, every loss was a failure. A failure to prevent the cruel twists and turns of fate that were sometimes visited upon good people.

'I... Thank you, Doctor. But in some ways, for me, it would have been a blessing.'

'In what way?'

Edward sucked in a gasp of oxygen from the mask before continuing. 'I've been alone for forty-seven years. Ever since my wife died.'

Tom looked away, feeling Edward's pain.

Naomi, watching him, realised he couldn't talk for a moment, so she answered the patient instead. 'I'm sorry to hear that. What happened?'

'Brain aneurysm. She was quite young when it happened. Only thirty-six. We'd not been married long. But she was my dream. My love. I could have met her again today.'

'You didn't remarry?' She stroked the patient's hand reassuringly with her thumb.

'No. My Betty was the only woman for me.'

Tom stared at the patient. They'd been in almost the same situation, widowed at a young age. But Edward Stovey had spent the majority of his life alone. Tom was still in the early stages of that path.

He wondered how Edward had coped. He felt suddenly full of questions he wanted to ask this man. But now was not the time. Their patient needed to be transferred up to the cardiac ward so that he could rest and be cared for properly.

He glanced at Naomi. 'I want half-hourly obs on Mr Stovey, please, Nurse.'

'Of course.'

Working with her in a desperate situation had been easy. They'd both known what had to be done. Their communication had been minimal, precise. Completely work related. But now their patient was in a better place and there wasn't the same kind of urgency, even though Mr Stovey's condition was still critical for the next twenty-four to forty-eight hours. The chances of another attack, maybe one even worse, were high. But now the immediate crisis was over, it was difficult to talk to Naomi again.

Tom couldn't be relaxed with her. It led to dangerous places, uncertain futures, pain and grief and guilt. Kissing her had been wrong. He knew it had been wrong, yet still it had been both amazing *and* terrifying.

He went over to the desk to quickly fill in his report on Mr Stovey so that a complete set of notes could travel up with the patient to the cardiac unit. He placed a quick call through to the ward that would take him and gave a potted history. Luckily they had a bed free and waiting. Once the notes were done, he would be able to call the porters to come and take Mr Stovey away.

Suddenly he sensed that Naomi was near him. He felt her rather than saw her there, and he turned to see her standing behind him, looking at him, as if contemplating whether to speak to him.

He bit the inside of his lip. 'Thank you for your help just then. I appreciate it.'

'No problem. It's what we're both here for.'

He couldn't drag his eyes away from her. It was like she had this magnetic pull over him.

What am I doing to myself? Putting myself through this torture?

He remembered that she'd agreed to go to the Spring Ball with Stefan. Unable to block out their conversation, he'd heard them arranging it. And the fact that there was a vacant flat in Stefan's block.

She's going to leave.

It had to be the best thing all round. Didn't it?

Tom turned away and went back to his paperwork. There was no point in going over it all. There was nothing he could do. Nothing he could offer her. At least, not what she deserved anyway. She was a wonderful person who deserved happiness and love. Two things he wasn't capable of giving her.

'I was thinking about what Mr Stovey said.' Her voice interrupted his train of thought.

'Oh?'

'Yes. About being alone for all those years.'

Tom signed his name on the paper, but didn't turn around. 'That's his choice.'

'Yes.' She came and stood by his side, laying her hand upon his to still the pen. He looked up into her stunning eyes. 'He *chose* that. I wonder if he was ever given another option.'

Then she walked back over to the patient's bed.

Tom watched her go, still feeling the intense heat upon his hand where she'd touched him and wondering what she'd meant. Had she been trying to imply something when she'd wondered if Mr Stovey had had another choice?

Was she implying that *he* had another choice?

Could she have been trying to say that, even though she'd agreed to go to the ball with Stefan, even though she was moving out, *they* still had another option as to how this could end?

He wasn't sure he could envision an alternative.

He returned to his paperwork, but he couldn't concentrate. He kept looking up at her, then at his patient. And back to her again.

Maybe she was right.

But what if she was wrong?

Two days later, Tom checked up on Edward in the cardiac unit. His patient was doing well, becoming more mobile and eating well.

The nurses informed him that Edward had had no visitors and no one had called to check on him either. That news had disturbed him the most.

He wondered how Edward was so alone. Surely a man in his eighties had friends or neighbours who would want to know how he was doing.

So he went to see the patient himself, waiting beside his bed for the older man to stir from his sleep. 'Good morning,' he said, when Edward blinked his eyes and pulled himself into an upright position.

'Morning. Dr Williams, isn't it?'

Tom nodded. 'How are you feeling?'

'I'm feeling good, I think. The doctors say I can go home soon.'

'That's excellent news. I'm really pleased to hear it.'

'Me too.'

'Yes? I'm glad. Do you have anyone that might help look after you when you get back?'

Edward shook his head. 'I look after myself.'

'No neighbours or family to check on you?'

'I'm on my own. I prefer it that way.'

'How long has it been that way?' Tom asked, genuinely interested.

'Ever since my wife died. She was all I ever needed in life. Since she passed, I've pretty much kept myself to myself.'

'Wasn't that lonely?'

'No. I had my work. I kept busy.'

'What did you do?'

'I was a taxi driver. Always with people, but, then again, always alone. But that was fine. It kept me busy and I could work for as long as I liked.'

Tom nodded uncomfortably, seeing too many similarities with his own life. Did he really want to be like Edward Stovey, working until his heart gave up? Then, what would happen when he *couldn't work*? Or when retirement loomed? How would he keep busy then? Tend a garden? Take up bingo?

'You never thought to remarry?'

Edward shook his head vehemently. 'There was only ever one woman for me. One true love. She was my soulmate, Doctor. You don't ever get to find another once you've lost them.'

He nodded. That was what he himself had always said. And he still believed that. How could he pursue something with Naomi when he knew it could never be the same as what he'd had with Meredith? Meredith had been his one true love, just as Betty had been Edward's.

Tom wondered if there was a chance they could be wrong. What if there was another person for you, as Naomi believed? What if that was true, but he didn't bother to look for her, or dare to take the risk? Would he be doomed to live like Edward? He shuddered at the thought of ending up in a hospital bed one day, with no one to care for him.

'How did you know Betty was your soulmate?'

Edward smiled. 'That's not an easy thing to answer. It's different for everyone. But for me, it was because Betty was in my thoughts all the time. She made me feel good. Alive. She made me laugh and she made me cry. When I wasn't loving her, I was worrying about her, or arguing with her, or laughing with her. I wanted to care for her. I wanted to be there for her. I wanted to take away her pain. I wanted to always see her smile. That's what it was like for me.' He looked at Tom. 'Do you have that with someone? Because if you do, then you should embrace it. Accept it. Love is a precious gift not always given to all.'

Tom sat back in his chair and thought hard. Yes, he'd had that with Meredith. All of it. But he was confused, because he'd also experienced it all with Naomi.

He didn't know how that was possible. Naomi was constantly in his thoughts, especially because he was trying his hardest *not* to think about her. She made him smile and laugh and he felt comfortable with her. Safe. Despite her clumsiness and her inability to climb ladders, cook safely or stay upright on four wheels. He cared for her and he didn't want to hurt her. But she was moving on. Agreeing to a date with Stefan. Looking for her own place to live.

By kissing her that night, by allowing himself that momentary weakness, hadn't Tom hurt her already? Their relationship had already been affected by that one act and he knew she had to be hurting because he was in pain, too. He'd kissed her and now he was enforcing this distance between them, because he thought that was the right thing to do. He'd thought that if he stayed away from Naomi, then he couldn't hurt her any more.

Because they couldn't have a future.

Could they?

No.

Tom shook his head and abruptly stood up. All this uncertainty, this toing and froing, was giving him a headache. He forced a smile and held out his hand to shake Edward's. 'Well, I just thought I'd come check on you. See how you were doing.'

'Well, I appreciate that, Doc.' Edward took his hand. 'Thanks for saving my life. You thank that pretty nurse for me, too.'

'No problem. Take care, Mr Stovey.' He started to walk away and just as he reached the ward entrance he heard Edward call out, 'Dr Williams?'

He turned. 'Yes?'

'I may be wrong, of course. There was someone I could have been with. *After* Betty. I liked her very much and we could have been happy.'

Tom stared at the man, not knowing what to say.

'I clung to my beliefs because I wasn't ready to let go of my wife. I knew that if I let her go, then I wouldn't have a direction. I wouldn't have a reason. I became so entrenched in my role as a grieving widower, I forgot that I could actually be someone else.'

Tom saw the meaningful look in his patient's eyes and understanding dawned on him. He also had two choices. One—take a chance on Naomi and challenge his theory about true love. Or two—remain as Meredith's widower for the rest of his life.

In one lay an opportunity for happiness, the other would lead to a life of loneliness and heartache.

'I saw the looks you were giving that nurse, but I also saw how she looked at you. There's love there, isn't there?' Mr Stovey smiled.

It seemed a simple choice.

Naomi watched as Tom walked straight past her without acknowledgement. Without a smile. He was fully focused, head down, reading a file as he walked, his brow lined in thought.

She missed him and she had no idea how that was even possible. They'd only been friends and flatmates for six weeks and yet she missed his smiles, the way he'd listen to her chat as they cooked together, the way he'd steal glances at her when he thought she wasn't looking.

The kiss they'd shared had been amazing. It had been the best kiss she'd experienced in her whole life and yet… she hated it. She hated it for taking Tom from her.

He'd retreated from her. They'd still shared a car into work and the same flat space, but that had been all. The conversations had gone, the caring had disappeared. In fact, any interaction between them had been non-existent.

Surely there had to be a way back for them. She'd meant for the roller derby to be fun, and at first it had been. They'd laughed *so* much. She could see him now, holding her hand, laughing, his eyes sparkling, as they'd both stumbled around.

How could she get that Tom back?

Naomi picked up the next patient file card and went to the waiting area to call her next patient through. 'Amy Smith?'

A middle-aged woman got up and smiled at her and she led her new patient through to a cubicle, pulling a curtain closed behind them.

'Take a seat. Right! Can you confirm your address and date of birth for me?'

Amy confirmed the details.

'Okay. So you've received an electric shock, is that right?'

Amy nodded emphatically. 'That's right.'

'Tell me what happened.'

She took a deep breath. 'Well! Lee has been renovating the house, but you know what men are like. They start a million jobs all at once instead of just doing one and doing it well. I'd been asking him to do the light switches for ages—we've barely had any proper electricity for a few weeks and he promised he'd do it, only he hadn't got round to it, so I had a go.'

'And what happened?' Naomi smiled through the explanation, cutting to the heart of the matter.

'I asked him to turn off the electricity and he said he would, but he disappeared off into the kitchen. So I thought he'd done it, only he hadn't, and when I went to touch the switch with my screwdriver I got this shock and got thrown back a bit.'

Naomi raised her eyebrows. 'Okay. Which hand received the shock?'

'My right, I suppose, but both hands were on the screwdriver.'

'Can I see?' She examined her patient's hand, but there were no burn signs or entry points to be seen, so that was good news. 'How far were you thrown back?'

'About a metre. I say "thrown"…it might just have been me staggering back, but I felt *something* and Libby who lives next door said I ought to come and get checked out in case the current passed through my heart or something.'

Electric shocks could be tricky. The effects weren't always immediately obvious and the more serious shocks could cause electroporation, where cell rupture caused tissue death.

In general, Amy seemed fine, but Naomi knew it was best to check her over just to make sure. 'I'll need to do an ECG, Amy. Have you had one before?' Her patient shook her head. 'It's a series of electrodes that I place mainly on your chest and it'll record an accurate trace of the electrical impulses in your heart. It'll just make sure everything's normal and it only takes a few seconds. In fact, it takes longer to set it up.'

'Right. That's fine. So you think I'm okay?'

'We'll do the trace just to make sure. Have you had any side effects? Nausea? Confusion? Pain?'

'Nothing.'

'You didn't pass out?'

'No. I've been fine.'

'We'll do the trace and make sure, then. Can you remove your top half for me?'

Amy began taking off her top. 'This is all Lee's fault. I swear, men are more trouble than they're worth! I don't see a ring on your finger, Nurse. I hope that means you're single?'

She nodded. 'I am.'

'Take my advice and stay that way. I wish I had. I would have been a lot happier. And my house wouldn't be such a mess either.'

'I…er…need to get the ECG machine. I'll be back in a tick.' Naomi slipped out of the cubicle and let out a deep breath. Maybe Amy was right. She should stay single and then she'd only have to worry about herself. Look at the mess she'd got into just because she'd kissed Tom. It hurt not being close to him any more and the pain was almost physical.

But that doesn't stop me wishing we had something more…

She pushed the machine back to the cubicle, closed the curtain once more and performed the trace. Amy's heart was fine. But she gave her an information sheet of things to look out for and sent her on her way.

'Thank you, Nurse. Let's see if I've got electricity when I get back!'

Naomi imagined that she would have. Amy might have complained about 'her Lee', but Naomi would still bet anything that she loved him. That she'd be heartbroken if there was something seriously wrong with him, or if he tried to leave her.

Or if he completely cut her off. The way Tom had done to her.

That's obviously what he wants. He's given me a clear message that he doesn't want anything to do with me any more.

Admitting that caused a pain in her chest and she had to stand there and rub at her breastbone for a moment, until it went away.

CHAPTER EIGHT

NAOMI SET OFF the next morning with more of a spring in her step, determinedly telling herself inwardly that what she was doing was the right thing. She'd spent a restless night tossing and turning, agonising over her decision. She knew she had to move out, find her own place and stand on her own two feet, as she'd promised herself she would.

Outside, it was slightly overcast as she walked purposefully to the bus stop and stood waiting, checking to make sure she had the right change. The sky darkened even as she stood there and she glanced up at it, worrying, realising she had misjudged the weather and hoping the downpour would hold off until later.

Her wish wasn't granted. As the bus took her to her destination the heavens opened and she knew that without an umbrella she was going to get soaked in just her small jacket.

Oh, well, she thought. She was only meeting a lettings agent after all.

She walked with her head down against the rain, as she headed for Echo Road where the flat was situated. From what she knew it was in a block of rather old flats. The flat she was looking at today had recently become empty after the tenant who had lived there for many years had passed away. The previous tenant had not decorated or touched the place since the seventies, the agent, Deanna, had said, but Naomi pushed that thought to one side. The important thing was that she could afford this flat. Decor could always be changed. Walls could be painted. As long as it was clean, she didn't mind.

By the time she got to the flats, her hair was plastered to her face and her clothes were soaked, her wet skirt constantly wrapping itself around her thighs.

Deanna was waiting for her and let her in exclaiming, 'Oh, look at you! You're like a drowned rat! At least you'll be able to dry off for a bit inside.'

Naomi managed a weak smile and followed her in.

The flat was dark with a weird orange wallpaper adorning the walls and she looked around disappointedly at the dark brown carpet and curtains. The kitchen was a melamine nightmare and the bathroom had an avocado-coloured suite and a discoloured linoleum floor. It smelt all musty, too. As if the place had been shut up for months, not weeks.

'It needs some modernisation, obviously,' Deanna said. 'But with a lick of paint and a bit of elbow grease, this place could be a stunning apartment. The sash windows are a real highlight and you could really make a feature of them. Maybe with some white voile and a bit of window cleaner.' Deanna laughed good-naturedly.

She was being optimistic, Naomi thought. The place needed a bit more than a lick of paint. The previous tenant had been a smoker, judging by the odd tinge of yellow to most things. However, she could see that with a bit of hard work and an awful lot of time she could probably make something of the place. Sadness washed over her as she pictured herself being here. She imagined her hair all tied up in a scarf to protect it, whilst she scrubbed and polished, with the windows open wide to air the place, to get rid of that stale smell.

It wasn't great. It wasn't what she wanted. But it would get her away from Tom and all the problems that came with living in his space. She had no choice. It was the middle of March now and she'd been living at Tom's for too long. If she were to live free of Tom and her feelings for him, then she'd have to move out of the beautiful flat she was in at the moment and take this place instead.

Sighing, she nodded to Deanna. 'I'll take it.'

The agent looked surprised. 'Great! I'll get everything in motion. The landlord will need a deposit and the first month's rent in advance.'

'Fine. I'll call you later and arrange it.'

'Fantastic!' She shook Naomi's hand. 'I'm sure you'll be very happy here!'

She smiled back at her. But it was forced. She could only hope that Deanna was right.

'This is Andi, sixteen years of age and, around two o' clock this afternoon, she took a heroin overdose. We've administered naloxone and given oxygen.' The paramedics gave them the rundown as they helped to slide the young girl onto the bed.

Naomi looked at her, feeling sympathy for the young girl. She wondered if the girl had meant to take the overdose, or if she'd not truly known what she was doing. Whatever the case, the medication was just starting to take effect and she was coming round.

Blinking heavily, Andi looked around her and then she suddenly sat up and hauled herself over the side of the bed.

'Where do you think you're going, young lady?' Tom said as he managed to grab her, and Naomi lowered the rail so they could get their patient back onto the bed.

She was glad Tom was there, because she didn't think she would have physically handled the girl on her own. She was taller than Naomi and quite broad.

'Get off me! Don't touch me!' The girl yanked her arm away from Tom and he backed off, with his hands raised as if in surrender.

'Okay, okay…' He looked over at Naomi. 'I've got her parents' details here, I'm just going to give them a ring. Can you do her obs for me?'

'Sure.' This confirmed what Naomi had suspected, that Tom was happy to talk to her when they were working on cases, but that he stuck to the medical, through and through. She accepted it, but she also knew she had to tell him that she'd found a place to live and that she would be leaving at the weekend.

He was bound to be relieved. She couldn't imagine he would react in any other way, after the way he'd been acting lately.

She nodded and watched him walk over to the phone, but just when her back was turned the teenager bolted from the bed and shot through the double doors of the department.

'Tom!' she shouted as she ran after the girl. She knew she wouldn't get far. The drugs only had a temporary effect.

Andi blundered through A&E, pushing past staff as if she were running from an assassin, and then shot through the waiting room and out of the main door to freedom. It was impressive. Many people got lost in the maze of A&E corridors, but this girl had found her way out even half drugged.

Naomi ran through the doors leading to the outside world and blinked in the sunshine as she searched for Andi's figure. Then she spotted her, lying flat out on the grass by the waiting ambulances. She knelt down beside her.

Andi was out cold.

Tom caught up with Naomi and came to stand over them both. 'How is she?'

'Unconscious, but there's a strong pulse.'

'Let's get her back inside and she can sleep it off.' He signalled for help to a paramedic who was restocking his ambulance with oxygen and BVMs and together, using a trolley, they got the girl back inside. Once Andi had been parked in a bay and her obs had been done to make sure she was okay, Naomi turned to Tom and laid her hand on his arm before he could walk away.

'Tom?'

He stopped in his tracks and turned around reluctantly. 'Yes?'

'I've found a place to live. The flat in Stefan's block. I viewed it yesterday and I can move in on Saturday.'

'I see.'

She waited to see if he would give any other reaction. 'I thought maybe I could cook for you on the Friday night… One last dinner together?' It would mean a lot to her if they could part as friends. Perhaps he would even be more at ease in her company if he knew that she was going.

'I'll cook. My treat,' he added, although he didn't look as thrilled by the news as she'd imagined he would. She watched him walk away and wondered if it had really been sadness she'd seen in his eyes, or whether it had all been in her own imagination.

Was this really their last night together?

Naomi sat in her bedroom, deciding upon what to wear. Tom was already busy in the kitchen and the aromas drifting around the flat were mouth-wateringly good.

No fire alarms had gone off, of course, as he was cooking, but there were the dulcet tones of classical music playing from the speakers in the living room.

Naomi wanted to make their last night special. This was their goodbye to one another, after all that had happened after that first clumsy fall off the ladder. Had that really been six weeks ago? She had only meant to have stayed one night, and now a month and a half later...

It really was time for her to go! *Talk about outstaying your welcome...*

She perused the dresses in her wardrobe, allowing her fingers to fondly stroke the dress she'd worn to the Phoenix riverboat restaurant. No, she wouldn't wear that one. She wanted something different. Something a bit more... grown up.

She selected a dark green wrap-around dress, then sat in front of the mirror and took her hair up with a few pins and twists. She applied some mascara and lipstick and spritzed herself with her favourite perfume.

Then, taking a deep breath, she went back into the main living area to see what Tom was cooking.

He stood slicing vegetables, dressed in a beautifully white shirt with dark trousers. He looked up as he saw her approach, his eyes widening for a brief moment.

'You look...nice,' he said, after a moment.

She'd take nice. At least he was *being nice* to her, she supposed, but, then again, she was going to be moving out in the morning. 'Thank you. So do you.'

He began chopping some nuts.

'What's on the menu?'

'A cranberry-stuffed pork roast with seasonal vegetables and a classic lemon meringue for dessert.'

'Sounds wonderful.'

'It'll be about an hour. Can I pour you a drink?'

'I'll have whatever you're having.'

She wandered away from the kitchen area and found herself over by the piano. The cleaner had been yesterday and in the vase sat a beautiful bouquet of delicate pink roses. She stroked the top of the instrument, sad that she'd never managed to hear him play, and realised he'd spotted her doing so. He quickly looked away and busied himself in the kitchen again, pretending that he hadn't seen.

Moving away, she went over to the sofa and sank onto it, tucking her feet up beside her as Tom brought her over a glass of white wine. She thanked him.

'My pleasure,' he said. He was about to head back to the kitchen, when she reached forward and took his hand.

'Tom…'

His pained expression met her gaze and then he looked away, biting his lip. 'What is it?'

'Sit with me. Just for a moment.'

He seemed to think about it briefly, but then he did as she asked and she let go of his hand, allowing him to sit back and be relaxed. She didn't like being the cause of his pain.

'I wonder if we could forget the last week or so. The atmosphere between us…it's been…difficult. I'd really like our last night together to be an enjoyable one. For both of us. Could we do that?'

Tom looked at her and there was such a mix of emotion on his face. Pain. Regret. And something else that she just couldn't pinpoint.

This was all so strange for her. These strong emotions were so new. She'd never felt so pained before, except maybe for that day when Vincent had finally passed, but even then there had been a small measure of happiness in that moment because she'd been so relieved that he was finally free of his prison. His skeleton had betrayed him and had kept him a prisoner within a body that had no longer worked properly. He'd even been unable to talk towards the end and they'd spent their last few hours together just holding hands, waiting for the darkness to fill his eyes, and when it had… When it finally had, it had almost been a blessing.

But this… These emotions she was experiencing with Tom were so totally different. There was no skeleton keeping Tom prisoner. But his memories, his emotions, were doing the same thing. She really didn't want to make him feel as if he was betraying his wife's memory.

'Since the…what happened between us…I've felt…distanced from you and that's been hard for me. I felt like we were good friends before.'

'We are.'

'But since the kiss—'

'I'm sorry, Naomi. I'm sorry I made you feel like you weren't wanted, it's just…' Naomi could see he was struggling for the right words '…when I kissed you, I felt… different from how I'd expected to feel and I was overwhelmed with—'

'Guilt?'

He shook his head. 'No. Yes. I'd thought I was in control of my feelings. I'd told myself how my life was going to be and suddenly I was going against all of that. You were in my arms and I just *had* to kiss you, like I was drawn to you, like you were the air that I breathe.' He looked up at her and caught her gaze with his own.

She sucked in a breath, amazed at how wrong she'd been. He hadn't been feeling guilty about his wife at all. Instead, he'd felt guilt at a betrayal of himself. Guilt at losing control.

'I couldn't promise you a future. I was angry at myself for being weak and giving in to an impulsive urge.'

She laid her hand on his. 'Don't be hard on yourself. We were having fun. Laughing, skating, singing to the music—badly!' She smiled. 'We were close. Good friends. Sharing a good time.'

'It was more than that.'

She nodded. She'd been trying to make light of the situation, to let him off the hook, but he was being honest with her and she appreciated that.

'There's something about you, Naomi, that I can't resist, and that scares me.'

She stared back at him, feeling her heart pound and her blood race. She felt the same way about him, too. That was why his rejection of her had hurt so much. When he'd begun pushing her away, she'd found her mounting feelings for him hard to deal with. But if he had felt the same way, perhaps he'd been retreating from her for his own self-preservation... If he'd felt he could offer her nothing in the way of a future together, maybe he'd thought that it would just be better not to have been with her in the first place.

'I feel it, too,' she said softly.

'You do?'

She nodded.

'I've felt so bad over these past few days. It's been so hard to stay away from you.' He reached over and stroked her face and she had to fight the urge to turn and kiss his fingers. She *burned* for him. Despite everything that had happened. It was as if she'd been through a trial of separation. And now that they were close together again, on the same sofa, within touching distance, she was learning that her original desire was still there, if not stronger than before.

Absence makes the heart grow fonder.

Wasn't that right? Was her heart involved in all of this? Because if it was, then could this be the love that everyone talked about, sang about? That was a huge, scary prospect, because she'd never loved like this before. It was terrifying because, even if she loved him, she knew she couldn't have him. Tom had made that plain.

'We're together again now. For this last night. Let's make it perfect. Because I know that we both want each other to be happy.'

'I would never want to hurt you, Naomi.' He tucked a stray strand of hair behind her ear and she smiled, feeling tears prick her eyes.

'Then be my friend, if you can't be anything else.'

Tom wanted to take her in his arms there and then and kiss her until they were both falling into oblivion, but he didn't move. The power of his self-control surprised him, because he wanted more than anything to touch Naomi, hold her and kiss her.

Since their kiss he'd been tortured. He'd been almost sent crazy by his agonies of uncertainty, wanting to be with her, fighting against his mindset that he couldn't offer her anything. It had almost torn him apart.

He was starting to falter in his belief about there being only one true love for everyone. What if Naomi were right and there *was* another person out there who could be his soulmate? And what if Naomi was that person? And he was throwing their relationship away because he was so certain that it was only possible to love one person so much, so certain that all other relationships after Meredith would pale in comparison.

But who was to say that these 'paler' relationships were no good? That they weren't as valuable, weren't as enjoyable, weren't as *true*?

Because, damn, his feelings for Naomi felt strong! They felt as strong as anything he'd ever felt for Meredith and that scared the living daylights out of him. He still barely knew her! They'd lived together for the best part of a couple of months, but, really, that was nothing. What did that prove?

That I can't bear the idea of her moving out. That I can't stand this self-imposed prison I've created around myself.

He became aware that Naomi was staring at him, with eyes watery with tears, tears that *he'd* caused. He'd told her that he would never want to hurt her but he was still doing exactly that. And it was all because of his stupid rules!

I must be wrong, because Naomi feels so right!

She was *right there*. Right next to him. Within touching distance. He could wipe that tear from her cheek. He could wipe it away and kiss her again and throw away all those self-regulated chains that were holding him back. He could reach out to her and break free and—damn the rules!

He could make her feel better. Make *himself* feel better. He could be happy with Naomi if only he gave himself the opportunity.

He leaned forward and, closing his eyes, tenderly kissed away the tears on her cheek.

She sucked in a breath and he opened his eyes to look at her. They were just millimetres away, both of them holding back for just a second more, just a moment to make sure the other one wanted this as much as they did and then...

He pressed his lips to hers. His hands delved into her thick mane of hair, pulling it free of the pins and clips as it tumbled around her shoulders and down her back. Then suddenly he was tasting her and she tasted divine. She kissed him back fervently, her hands pulling him to her, pressing him against her as she lay back on the sofa and he enveloped her, his tongue exploring and his senses going into overdrive as he tasted, smelt, touched.

She groaned his name and reached for his shirt at his

waistband, pulling it up and free so that her hands could find his bare skin beneath.

He needed her. He needed her so badly and yet he had to be tender. She was so soft and delicate and he wanted to enjoy every sensation, every caress, to see her every delight, revel in her joy and her ecstasy.

Finding the knot of material at her waist, he tugged it free and began to remove her dress...

Naomi gloried in the delights befalling her body. Tom had an expert touch. He knew exactly where to touch her, where to taste, and his fingers played over her skin as if she were a finely tuned musical instrument.

Tom's mouth slowly tasted each breast, delicately licking and kissing her, trailing down over the gentle slope of her stomach, giving teasing little nips and licks, sending sensations of both shock and pleasure through her body, until finally his mouth came to settle between her thighs.

Arching her back, she groaned as he sought out her most delicate area. Grasping his hair in her hands, she gasped for breath, riding the waves of pleasure that sang their way through her nerve endings and sent her sensory system into overload, as her pleasure built and built until she was crying out his name, begging him to stop.

Was this what she had been missing all her life? This passion, this ardour? This frenzy of desire and want and need? She had dismissed such feelings as unimportant when she'd met and married Vincent, believing that the measured love she'd had for him would be enough to carry them through what was to come. She'd believed that her friendship with Vincent had been just as important as her love and that the heat, the fire, the intensity of all the feelings she was experiencing right now were something that she could live without.

She'd not known what she had been missing. Of course, she'd seen films where the two main characters got lost in a hot, scorching night, totally consumed by their passion for each other. But she'd dismissed them as *pretend*. They hadn't been real. Surely that wasn't what real people experienced. She'd thought it was impossible to find someone like that, someone who could make you go stir crazy in bed.

And so she'd continued to sit and watch the movies next to Vincent and had managed not to worry that she was missing out on something.

Now that she was experiencing it, she knew she couldn't live without it. If only she'd known…

Tom entered her and she closed her eyes in delight. This was *it*. This was the feeling that she'd read about, that she'd often wondered about, that she'd wanted to feel, but never had. This feeling of being consumed, of being filled, of being joined to another in such an intimate way. And it was wondrous! Being with Tom, knowing that he needed her as much as she needed him, made her feel so free. It was crazy, laugh-out-loud amazing.

She could feel Tom's ardour increasing as his movements got faster and harder. Gripping him to her, she gasped for air, feeling the hard strength of his taut body above her, riding her. His mouth found hers and then she lost herself yet again, allowing herself to fall into the wonderful chasm that was Tom's arms, letting go of everything about herself that she'd ever held back, encouraging him to do the same, until suddenly—wonderfully—he cried out, thrusting into her like his whole life depended upon it and then…then he stilled. Just for a moment. Then his mouth found hers once again, pressing his lips against hers. He continued kissing her, tasting her lips, her tongue, her neck, tracing her collarbone with his lips. His hot breath trailing along her skin made her tingle.

For a second, they just lay there, holding each other, still entwined.

Naomi revelled in this glorious sensation. She had found a new side of herself that she hadn't known existed. Never before had sex been anything like this. There'd been some drunken fumbling and Vincent had done his best to try and please her, but there'd been so many physical restrictions. With Vincent, the body had been something to fight against. For him to get angry at. He'd not been able to touch her the way she'd wanted. Not been able to excite her the way she'd really wanted.

It had always been a frustrating event and in the end something that they had stopped doing. Their marriage had become a friendship after that. It had been all about companionship and she'd lied and told herself that that was enough.

With Tom sex was something to be enjoyed. To be revelled in. She'd been made love to and she now knew it was wonderful. All her dreams about what it might be like, all her desires, had been fulfilled and she felt sated. She felt content.

And from somewhere, tears began to fall.

She couldn't help it. The tears came unbidden and poured from her like a bursting dam. Before she knew it, she was sobbing, curling in on herself. She felt her grief and her delight pummelling her alternately until she didn't know what she was crying about.

Tom looked at her, bewildered for a moment, but then he pulled her close, wrapping his arms around her, just holding her, waiting for whatever it was to pass.

'Hey, it's okay. Shh… Don't cry.' He stroked her arms, kissing her bare shoulders, then her cheeks and her eyelids.

He continued to be unbelievably kind as she lay there, until her tears were spent and dried upon her face. Then finally she lay still. She was afraid to look at him. Afraid of how he might react.

But he just held her, tightly, in his arms, her limbs still entwined with his. 'You okay?'

Naomi sniffed and nodded. 'Yes.'

'What was that all about?' he asked gently.

She stared at the wall, unable to look him in the eyes, but knowing she couldn't tell him what she was feeling. How she felt *loved*. She knew he wasn't ready to hear that. Not right now. 'I don't know.'

Tom frowned, but he kissed her one more time. 'Don't worry about it,' he said. He held her even closer, refusing to let go.

It was almost enough to make her cry again, but this time she was prepared. She was ready for the tears. They might have surprised her before, but she wasn't going to let that happen again.

She kissed his arm and laid her head against his chest, listening to his heart beat, falling in love with its rhythm. Falling in love with him.

She knew she was falling for him. She couldn't help it. Her emotions had always been quick to assert themselves. She'd always known that when she did, she would fall fast and hard. She was still wary. It had all gone so badly after they had only kissed. Now they'd made love. But maybe this was a good sign. She'd thought that Tom would be happy to get rid of her, but they had just made love in the most beautiful way...

Snuggling into his arm, she closed her eyes and imagined. She imagined a brilliant future for the both of them. Surely it had to go well from now on. Look at how well they fitted together. It felt *right*.

He kissed the top of her head and she turned to look at him. 'Okay?'

Tom smiled. 'I am. You know, I really ought to go and turn the food down. It's probably overcooked by now.'

Naomi laughed. He was even burning food like her. 'You should. But maybe you should bring some of it back here. I'm starving, suddenly.'

She saw his gaze travel to her lips and he kissed her once again. 'For food?'

'Amongst other things.'

He smiled. 'Well, maybe I could tempt you again with those…other things.'

Her hand slipped down his body. 'Tempt away.'

They made love once again and after, lying spent in each other's arms, their hunger for food overcame them. Naomi watched him walk away to the kitchen, tall and proud, admiring his broad back, neat waist, gorgeous bottom and long, powerful thighs. He was a beautiful man to look at but he was beautiful inside, too. He'd tried to stay away from her because he'd thought he had nothing to offer her, but he was wrong. He had everything to offer. She just hoped that he believed it now, too.

He came back into view with a towel around his waist and carrying a bedsheet for her. She took it, smiling, and stood up to wrap it around her body. 'Thank you.'

He smiled at her and dipped his head to kiss her again, his lips soft against hers. 'Can I get you anything? A drink? Something to eat?'

'Is dinner ruined?'

'It's rescuable. I think I might have carbonised the meat, though.' He gave a short laugh.

'As long as it's still edible, I could probably eat a horse.'

'Maybe we should get dressed, if we're going to eat?'

Naomi looked down at her bedsheet and his towel and grinned. 'Let's not.'

He laughed again and guided her over to the table. 'Take a seat. I'll serve.'

She sat patiently and waited, her olfactory senses suddenly going into overdrive at the aroma of the food, and her stomach rumbled.

When Tom brought dinner to the table, Naomi didn't think it looked burnt at all. The pork was perfect, with plenty of crackling, and the vegetables were soft and buttery just the way she liked. She'd always hated it when people served them al dente anyway.

It was a gorgeous meal, made better by the fact that she and Tom were at peace again. At least for the evening. Everything might change when she moved out. But hopefully, they were moving in the right direction. One with her and Tom together.

She raised her glass in a toast. 'To good food, good friends and love,' she said, impulsively.

He clinked his glass to hers. 'Good food, friends…and love.' He swallowed his mouthful of wine and gazed at her over the table thoughtfully.

Naomi had never expected the evening to go like this. They'd barely been speaking to each other at the start! But now they were close again and would hopefully remain that way. Even though she was moving out.

It was a grim thought, imagining the new flat. There was so much hard work she had yet to do in order to get it ready, to try and make it as wonderful as this. It was going to take a lot of time and she was going to miss living here. Tom had given her a truly wonderful gift by allowing her to share this beautiful space with him. By allowing her to share his life. His feelings. She glanced over at the piano and wondered. 'Tom…can I ask you a big favour?'

'Of course.'

'Before I go, would you…play for me? Play the piano?'

She saw him glance over at the instrument and take in a breath. He looked uncertain. He looked…doubtful. She wondered if she'd pushed him too far.

But he suddenly got up, brushed at his mouth with a napkin and walked over to the piano, staring down at it, as if he might be about to fight it. As if it were dangerous. But then he bent, pulled out the stool and lifted the lid as he settled onto the seat.

Naomi went over to him.

'What shall I play?'

'Whatever your heart tells you to.'

He glanced at her and nodded, raising his hands over the keys before finally, all of a sudden, he touched them and began to play.

The next morning, when Tom woke, he instantly looked to his side and saw Naomi sleeping. She looked so beautiful. Peaceful. With her face in gorgeous repose, her lips looked so soft and her naked body beneath the sheets was so tempting.

It had been a long time since he'd woken up with a woman beside him. The last time had been with Meredith and he'd never expected anyone to take her place, but suddenly there was…

Naomi Bloom.

What the hell do I do now?

Naomi had even mentioned love. It had just been a toast, but he wondered if she had read something into their relationship. He wasn't sure he was ready for that. It was a huge leap from friendship to love, and one he wasn't certain he could offer.

He wanted to give her everything. Very much so. But

love? He didn't know where he stood on that issue. And Naomi deserved to have someone who loved her and who could fully commit himself to her.

Could that person be him?

He had feelings for her, yes. There was no denying that. Making love to her had been amazing, deep and intense, but he wasn't sure he was ready to fully hitch his wagon to someone else just yet and give himself so completely. If he did that, if he could do that... He had no idea what would happen if he lost her. Would he be able to go through that turmoil again?

There must be an opportunity here to take things slowly. Naomi would be moving out later today, after her shift, and that would create some much-needed space between them. It would allow them both to get some perspective after living and working in each other's pockets over the last month or so. Judging by Naomi's tears, it wasn't just him who was feeling overwhelmed. He wasn't sure what to think about that. Although she hadn't seemed upset, so much as thoughtful. It didn't seem that the experience had been awful for her.

Their coming together had been something that neither of them had been able to resist. The moment had seemed primal, soulful. But in speaking those words in her toast, Naomi had imbued it with so much meaning. Did she think that Tom *loved* her? Because he couldn't promise her that.

He climbed out of bed, being careful not to wake her, and opened the door of his wardrobe. There, on the top shelf, was his one remaining photo of Meredith. It had been taken on their wedding day. She looked out at him from the frame, her head tilted slightly to one side, as if questioning him.

Why is there another woman in my place, Tom?

Her beautiful face amongst the flowers in her head-dress and veil was a vision in white. He'd known exactly what he was doing when he'd married Meredith and he'd known exactly what he could offer her. He had been certain. But with Naomi...

What have I done?

Tom closed the wardrobe door and sank his head against the wood. He'd made a dreadful mistake. What he'd done had not been fair to either of them. He'd allowed his physical urge to be with Naomi to override his logical thought processes. The ones that had told him to hold back, to keep a safe distance from her. He'd let Naomi think that there could be a future for them both and that simply wasn't fair.

He needed to tell her the truth. He owed her that much.

He went out into the living area and instantly his gaze fell to the piano. He'd even *played* for her. He was such a fool.

He knew they needed to talk. He needed her to wake up, so that he could tell her. So that he could let her know that this was something that would have to be taken slowly or not at all. That this wasn't love. Not yet. Even if she thought it was.

Tom sat on the sofa and waited.

Naomi woke and rose, grabbing a robe from the back of the bedroom door. All her clothes were in her room. This morning she felt good. Great, even. She and Tom had healed the rift between them and in the bargain she'd also discovered what it was in life that she had always been missing. Amazing passion, intensity, love.

It didn't matter that she was moving out today. The distance might even be a good thing, giving each of them their own space and putting the relationship on an equal footing. They would be able to date properly, Tom calling round to her, picking her up and taking her out. Their relationship would start just as any other one would. They would start separately, until that moment, when, if everything went right, they would come together and unite, be one.

She used Tom's small en-suite, splashing some water on her face and drying it before she headed out of the bathroom and into the living space. She smiled when she saw him, ready to wish him good morning.

Tom stood there, by the piano, and it seemed he had been waiting for her. He'd changed into his usual suit and still looked just as magnificent dressed as he did naked.

I'm a really lucky girl.

'I don't think we should do this any more.'

She was rocked to her very core. What? What did he mean? Had she missed something? Had something happened whilst she'd slept?

'You deserve someone who can offer you the world, Naomi. You deserve someone who can fully love you as you deserve to be loved. Until I know if I'm that man, I don't think we should...do that again.'

She wasn't sure what to say. She deserved love, yes, but so did he. She knew she could love him, and in fact, she knew she probably already did.

But he'd said he wasn't sure he could be the man for her. That he thought they needed to *wait* until he worked out whether he could be with her. Naomi wondered if this was some sort of a cruel joke. She didn't know what to think. She wouldn't put up with it; she wouldn't wait any longer. Not now she knew. Not now she knew what love could be like. The way it *felt*.

'And I'm supposed to just hang around until you work that out?'

'I think we might have rushed—'

'How dare you, Tom? How dare you? I've been nothing

but straight with you! I've held nothing back from you from the start and what…is that suddenly too much for you?'

He remained calm as he answered her, as if patiently explaining something to a child. 'We made love, yes, and that was great, but that didn't mean…I can't *love* you, Naomi, the way you expect me to. I just think we should hold back for a bit.'

'Do you?' she asked, suddenly furious! She couldn't believe he was doing this to her. Only last night, she'd been on cloud nine! How could he be so hot one moment and so cold the next?

'Well, hold back all you want, Tom, but I'm not going to. Life is for living and for being happy! I thought I was going to spend it with you, but if you're going to suddenly tell me to "hold your horses", then I'm getting off this ride. I've done the waiting game. I've been there, done that, and I'm not doing it again for anyone! You either love me or you don't.'

She waited for his response. She'd not meant to say it straight out like that. Although she didn't think it was that hard, to be honest. She knew how she felt, but if he didn't know, then…

Don't cry again.

She could feel the tears welling. She could feel them burning the backs of her eyes as she stood there, challenging him, but she refused to blink, holding them back.

When it became clear that Tom *couldn't* answer her, Naomi stormed into her room and slammed the door. Slumping onto her bed, she began to cry, pulling her pillow over her head so that Tom wouldn't hear.

CHAPTER NINE

NAOMI SAT HUDDLED in the staffroom. She'd checked the rota. She was on duty till four p.m. So was Tom. They had a whole day to spend together after last night. After their conversation that morning.

How can I look him in the eye?

She couldn't picture it. She couldn't imagine him wanting to spend even a tiny second alone with her, after what had happened. She wanted to be a million miles away.

How could she and Tom work together in A&E without it spilling over and affecting everyone else they worked with? What about their patients? She didn't know if it was possible.

She thought back to last night, to the moment where she'd cried in Tom's arms. He had made love to her as if she were the most amazing person he knew. As if she were precious and he never wanted to let her go. He'd made her feel special, important. As if she mattered. As if she were someone who deserved every moment of happiness he could give her.

And then that happiness had been crushed!

She sank her head into her hands and groaned out loud, just as Stefan came in with Jackie.

'Oh, dear! Rough night, was it? Need the hair of the dog?' Stefan joked.

She looked at him and sighed, shaking her head. 'No. It wasn't booze.'

'Right. Another man, then? Or did you get to the last episode of your favourite box set?'

She smiled and shook her head. It wasn't as if she could tell them what had happened. 'Something like that.'

'Well, you and Dr Williams must be watching the same box set, then, because his face doesn't look much better this morning, either!' As she spoke Jackie turned to put her coat in her locker, so she didn't see the look that crossed her friend's face.

Naomi wondered how bad Tom was feeling. She'd made her own way into work, so she hadn't seen him since she'd left this morning. She was still moving out this afternoon; everything was set.

She wondered if the atmosphere would be as bad as it had been after the kiss. Or worse. Then he'd just been standoffish. Distant. Polite. Terse. She fervently hoped that what they'd done last night wouldn't affect everyone else around them. They all had to work together. And a disrupted team in A&E did not bode well for the rest of the hospital.

But how could she face him after their confrontation this morning?

'Where is he?' she asked, trying to sound casual.

'Oh, talking to Matron, I think.'

She got up to look through the glass in the staffroom window and saw him talking to the matron across the department. He looked awful. He was a little pale and there were shadows under his eyes. A sickly heaviness weighed upon her, but then he turned and noticed her watching and he suddenly stood up taller. He finished his conversation with the matron and then he walked away, without looking back.

Her heart sank.

* * *

He'd wanted her. Pure and simple. It had been an agony to keep himself away from her, despite all his attempts to keep distance between them. Naomi Bloom had got under his skin. There was something about her that he just couldn't ignore.

Being with her last night had been... He sighed. There were no words to describe adequately the way he'd felt. And those moments afterwards, as they'd just lain in each other's arms, had been perfect until she'd cried...

Tom shook his head angrily. She'd got under his skin. And there was a chance she thought he *loved* her!

He couldn't let her believe that. He *couldn't*!

He couldn't let it be true.

Because if he let it be true, then he'd be going against his own vow. His promise to never love another because...

If I allow her in, if I let her get close and then I lose her, like I lost Meredith...

He rubbed at his eyes and sank back against the wall. He just couldn't do it. He'd taken things too far. He should never have slept with Naomi. Everything was complicated. He still had to see her every day at work, but now everything would be different.

That was one of the things he'd been afraid of from the very beginning. He should have made sure they stayed just friends. He should have rescued her from ladders and drunks and left it at that.

But he hadn't.

He'd got involved and, not only had he upset himself, but he'd also upset her. Had made Naomi feel things that she should have been protected from.

Tom sank down the wall until he was crouching and stared at the people that walked past, looking at him, concerned.

It had all gone so terribly wrong.

* * *

Naomi stood back as the paramedic wheeled in the young woman on the back board.

'This is Alison, twenty-one years of age, and the victim of a car-versus-cyclist incident. She was cycling along the main road, when a car swerved and hit her from the side. The vehicle was travelling at about thirty-five miles an hour. She was wearing this.' The paramedic showed them the cracked cycle helmet and Naomi winced at the damage, then her wince quickly turned to a frown as she noticed Tom enter Resus.

The paramedic continued, 'Head to toe, we have a scalp laceration in the right occipital region, neck pain with a score of seven, a suspected fracture of the right humerus and clavicle, a suspected fracture of the right femur and general cuts and scrapes down the right side. BP is one twenty over seventy, pulse is one ten and she has a BM of four point two. Pain relief was offered, but refused.'

Tom pulled on gloves and tied an apron around his waist. Studiously, he seemed to ignore her. 'Let's get her off the back board, please.'

They all worked together to roll the patient, sliding her out from the back board. Then the paramedics left and the team could continue monitoring the patient.

Naomi leaned over her, so Alison could see a friendly face. She looked scared and her long blonde hair was slightly matted with blood. 'Hi, Alison, I'm a nurse. I'm going to help look after you. Now you might hear a lot of noise, or feel some pushing or pulling, but we'll talk you through it all, okay?'

'Yes.' Alison tried to nod, but winced.

'Now, where do you hurt the most?'

'My leg and my arm.'

The paramedics had put both of her limbs into splints

and Naomi knew they'd have to wait for the X-rays before anything more could be done.

'Can you tell me where you are?'

'In hospital.'

'And what day is it?'

She told her.

'Okay. Are you allergic to anything, Alison?'

'No.'

Naomi proceeded to test Alison's blood pressure, whilst the rest of the team buzzed over her like bees, checking, testing, assessing. They got IV access and did a quick scan of her abdomen, whilst someone else checked her pupil dilation and tracking. Naomi couldn't help but notice old track marks on Alison's arms, indicating a history of drug abuse. But they were old, nothing recent. Perhaps that explained her reluctance to use the pain relief offered by the paramedics.

'Am I going to die?' Alison asked.

Naomi leant over her again. 'No, you're not going to die, Alison. It looks like you've maybe broken your arm and leg.'

Alison began to cry. 'He hit me. I can't believe he hit me!'

Naomi glanced at Tom, before she could stop herself. Here was a woman who had been hit by a car, who was clearly going to survive. Tom's wife had not been so lucky. She wondered what it did do to him every time a patient like this came into Resus. The memories of what had happened to Meredith must hit him hard each and every time. Did he resent the fact they'd not been able to save her? Had he been angry?

Tom's face was stony and impassive. It gave nothing away. 'Let's get her to CT.'

The computerised tomography suite would give them

a much better view of what was going on inside Alison's body without submitting her to a full MRI. It combined X-ray technology with a computer to create images of the structures within the body, not only including bone, but also organs and blood vessels.

Naomi went with them to the CT suite and stood to one side as the radiographers gave Alison her instructions to lie still.

She waited behind Tom, glancing at him, wondering what he was thinking behind his stony facade.

He glanced at her briefly, then turned back to look at the first pictures of the scan coming through on the computer screen.

He wasn't willing to talk just yet.

Obviously what had happened between them had shocked him. It had shocked Naomi, too. She would never have thought she would have reacted that way. She had never felt that way with a man before. What she'd experienced with Tom, she had felt certain was love, but he seemed to be denying that that was possible. It seemed that he'd promised himself he would never fall in love again and he was standing by that promise.

And what about me? I said I'd never get involved with a man again. But I did and now look at what's happened!

She had been weak to allow Tom in. She had been stupid, allowing a man to tangle up her emotions, after she'd sworn to always protect her heart. She should have known better.

Alison's CT results came through clear. There was a small fracture of the humerus, near the shoulder, a stable fracture of the clavicle and a hairline fracture of the leg. No other internal injuries could be seen and, as her blood pressure was stable and her pulse steady, the neck brace was removed and she was allowed to sit up to have her scalp stitched. She didn't need surgery. She'd been incredibly lucky.

Tom sat next to the patient, perched on a stool, with the suture kit ready in his hand. Naomi stood beside him, cleaning the wound and soon it was ready for him to stitch.

'I've been so lucky, haven't I?' Alison asked.

Naomi nodded. 'You have. Incredibly lucky.'

'This could have been so much worse.'

She said nothing. This seemed a natural reaction for people in A&E who had had accidents. They played the 'what if?' question too readily.

'The driver was hurt, too. Was he brought here? Is he all right?'

'He was drunk,' Tom said, starkly, his voice terse, his mood impenetrable. 'But fine.'

Alison breathed out an audible sigh of relief. 'Thank goodness.'

'Thank goodness? He was drunk driving; he broke your arm and leg.'

Alison glanced over at Tom. 'I can't judge. I don't know him. Perhaps he had a reason for being drunk at that time of the morning. Maybe he'd been trying to drown his sorrows, or he'd lost someone he loved. He might even have an addiction. So, I can't judge him. Not me.'

Naomi finished clearing away the blood around the wound and stood there shocked at Alison's kindness. She knew most people would blame the driver, would talk about suing him. But this patient wasn't doing any of those things. She didn't even seem angry. 'You have a good way of looking at life, Alison.'

'You have to think of it that way. You can't be bitter about things that aren't in your control.'

Naomi thought that perhaps Alison was right. Maybe what had happened between her and Tom had never been in their control. Meeting him that first time had certainly been a complete accident, when she'd fallen from that stupid ladder. And then her flat had been burgled… Living in an awful bedsit had been her only choice, because she'd wanted to live in London. That choice had led to this moment. But she'd had no control over these odd events.

She'd chosen to never get involved with another man again. But despite her choice, her determination, it seemed fate had intervened. And now…

'Do you need me for anything else?' she asked Tom. She was only referring to the patient's care, but suddenly she was all too aware that it sounded like she was asking about life in general.

'No. I'm fine here,' he replied.

She nodded. Of course.

Tom finished the stitching swiftly and they covered the injury with a gauze pad. Naomi smiled at Alison.

'Do you need me to call anyone for you?'

The patient shook her head. 'There's no one.'

'Are you sure?'

'I'm all alone. But that's okay. Because then, I only have to worry about me.'

Naomi frowned. She'd been so sure when she'd arrived in London that alone was the best way to live. It seemed she had been right all along. It was like Alison said. It gave you less to worry about. There was less to mess up and there was no chance of disappointing anyone.

'Would you like a cup of tea?' she asked.

Alison nodded. 'I'd love one.'

Naomi found Tom at the drink station in the staffroom, just as he scooped his tea bag out of his cup and dropped it into the bin.

'Sorry to disturb you,' she said. 'I was just going to make Alison a cup of tea.'

He nodded and stepped aside to make room for her, ardently stirring his drink.

'I'll move out the second I get back this afternoon. You won't have to see me.'

'Naomi—'

'No, Tom...I can see you're uncomfortable and so am I. But don't worry. I'm sorting it all out.' She picked up Alison's drink and left before he could say anything else.

There! she thought. *Simple. Decisive. To the point.*

If she'd kept her distance in the first place then it would never have been a problem. So, now if Tom didn't want to be committed to her, then fine. She didn't need him. She refused to want him.

There would be no more Tom.

There would be no more Naomi and Tom.

There would be no more of that heat and need and wanting and wishing and...

Naomi handed the drink to Alison, smiling grimly, lost in thought.

There would be no more feeling lost.

How had she misunderstood so badly? The way he'd touched her, kissed her, caressed her—it had been as if he'd been holding a rare treasure, as if he couldn't believe he was allowed to touch something so valuable. At least that was what his eyes had said. It had been there in his face, in his body, too. Every part of him treating her like a precious jewel.

Maybe she had imagined it all.

Perhaps Tom had been right when he'd been talking about them making love. Perhaps it was just sex, nothing more. Perhaps what they'd done hadn't been special. After all, she didn't have another point of reference.

No. She shook her head. *No, there was something else there.*

No matter what had happened, however, it had definitely grown far too complicated. Tom had made it absolutely clear that he wasn't in the market for a relationship and that he could never love another.

His relationship with Meredith must have been something truly special. She must have been an angel for him to fall so deeply in love that he couldn't tolerate the idea of loving someone else.

Naomi wasn't sure if she even knew what love was any more.

She'd been determined not to say anything more to him, and had decided to walk away with her head held high. But then she'd seen him, standing alone outside, taking a breather between patients, and before she had known what she was doing she had walked over to him. She was overcome with a desire to explain, to try and put into words what she'd felt when she'd sobbed with happiness in his arms.

He looked up, surprised, as she opened her mouth and the words poured out.

'Last night, Tom…it meant something to me. It meant more than just two people coming together to rid themselves of their frustrations. It meant…*more.* I can only speak for myself, when I say this, but I'm angry at myself for letting it happen. Angry because it ruined the friendship that we had and turned it into something else. Something uncomfortable. Something painful. I know you regret it. But at the same time, for me, it was something joyous, something mind-blowing. It meant that my eyes were opened to a possibility that I could only have dreamed of… That moment brought me you. And believe you me,

I didn't plan this. Like you, I told myself I would never fall in love again. I told myself that real, burning, passionate love caused too much pain, too much suffering for it to ever be worth it. But with you, I trusted that it wouldn't happen. That you wouldn't hurt me—'

'Naomi—'

'But you *have* hurt me, Tom. In a way I hadn't even known I should be protecting myself from. The way I felt in your arms was something I'd never experienced before and that was why I cried... It was overwhelming. Overwhelmingly beautiful.'

'I—'

'I need to step away from you. You said you can't give me what I need and I understand that, I do. I never even knew that I needed it myself! But I think I do now. I want to be loved, Tom, and I don't think that should be something to be feared. You're not ready,' she said, faltering, with tears flowing freely down her face. She didn't care what she looked like any longer. 'But I can't hang around and keep torturing myself with the thought of what might have been every time I look at your face.'

She turned, desperately, and began to walk away, her head too full to think.

Tom called her name, but the pain in her chest hurt too much to turn around and listen to anything he might have to say.

What could he tell her that she didn't already know?

He couldn't love her the way she wanted him to.

So that had to be the end.

Last night, Tom...

It was hours after Naomi had left the hospital and still he couldn't get her words out of his head. She was right. It *had* meant something. He hadn't let himself acknowledge it at the time and had been too overwhelmed by her emotional outpouring but now, when he considered how she'd made him feel… He knew that it really had meant something.

Naomi was truly special. And therein lay the problem. Because Tom didn't want her to mean something. He didn't *want* to care deeply for her. He didn't want to be falling in love. Love only hurt. He'd learnt the hard way that life got in the way and that terrible accidents happened. What if Naomi was taken from him just as Meredith had been? If he let himself care for Naomi, *love* Naomi, then he knew he wouldn't cope with losing her. His fear of that would ruin everything. He'd been there already. He wouldn't go through it again. Couldn't go through it again.

He'd relied on his work since Meredith had died and that had seen him through. It was his way of continuing to connect with people. He could still help them, if only for a short time. A&E had been perfect because he was able to step in and make their lives better, and then his patients could be on their way. No one had to develop feelings and no one would get hurt. Tom had thought that he would be able to live the rest of his life at an emotional distance from everybody.

It was all a form of self-preservation. Surely everyone was guilty of it in one way or another. Was it so bad of him to put up walls in this way? He was protecting himself. He was protecting Naomi. But of course, he knew, she couldn't see that, that he was doing this for them both.

Tom didn't know what to think, except that he needed this whole situation to change. He needed…*damn it!* He needed Naomi!

He would give anything to call her back, and take her in his arms. He wanted to talk to her, about something, *anything*. He wanted to just *be* with her.

But he couldn't be with her. He wouldn't allow himself to do so. What had happened was for the best. Yes, it still hurt, but surely it was best to make that clean break now, before the hurt turned to agony.

He headed back into the department. It was technically the end of his shift, but he didn't care. He needed to work. He couldn't face the thought of going back to the flat, and seeing her emptying it of her things. If he worked, he wouldn't think about her. Or, at least, he'd try not to.

The rest of the staff were thrilled to see him return. They were overrun with patients and, for a brief hour or two, he managed to forget about her completely. He didn't have time to think about what had happened that morning, or what she'd said. In those few precious hours, he didn't have to think about that look on her face when she'd run from him.

But then, when he was told to take a break, the thoughts came clamouring in. He pushed them to one side, telling himself over and over again that he was doing the right thing. He figured that if he told himself enough times, he might even start believing it was true.

Naomi packed up the last of her things. Most of her possessions were now in boxes, or the suitcase she'd taken from her old flat, but she'd just needed to return to Tom's flat to collect her toothbrush and make-up from the bathroom.

Moving here in the first place now seemed like such a mistake. She'd been sucked in by how beautiful it all was. After her experience with the bedsit, she'd been happy to escape to such luxury. And, of course, then there'd been Tom, who had been the most wonderful feature of the flat.

But this had never been meant for her. She'd come out of a lonely childhood, into a lonely, strangely solitary marriage where it had seemed she had spent the entire time *waiting*. She had always been waiting for something bad to happen, another bone to grow, another injury to occur, as Vincent had steadily grown worse. She remembered the big grandfather clock in the hallway of their home and suddenly its loud ticking had never meant so much. She'd been stuck on pause. Trapped in a place from which she'd had no escape, and so she had waited, patiently, for the end.

Vincent's condition had called all the shots in their marriage. It had governed everything and at the time, she hadn't minded. She'd enjoyed looking after him, had enjoyed that they were so close and had accepted everyone's praise of her, the way they'd said she was *being so brave*. At least, she'd escaped her childhood, always determined not to be like her mother, flitting from one relationship to another, always searching, always falling for the prettiest face and getting hurt.

She knew she'd chosen Vincent because he had been safe. She could admit that to herself now. He had been dedicated to her. Dedicated to their relationship.

He'd *needed* her.

And she'd revelled in that role as the dutiful wife, for their time together, playing it safe right to the end.

Then she'd made her big move to the capital. Finally she had been able to stand on her own two feet, throw caution to the wind and enjoy life. She had told herself that she would push her nursing skills to the limits, make new friends and live a whole new life. Naomi had been determined to move onwards and upwards, enjoying her freedom, just as she'd promised Vincent before he'd died that she would.

But she'd met Tom and had fallen for him. She'd been enticed by his good looks, given herself to him, and just like her mother she'd ended up alone and hurting.

But today I start again.

Naomi rallied herself. She would call the last few weeks a false start. They were just a minor blip in her plan. This time, she would stubbornly remain single, at least for a while.

As she gathered up her things Tom's toothbrush suddenly seemed lonely in its pot, now that she had removed her own, and she gazed at it wistfully. They had been so good in their brief time together. But now she had to put Tom from her mind.

Naomi zipped up her toiletries bag and left.

An hour or so later she looked around her new flat, trying to find some kind of optimism. Luxury and opulence were not part of her normal world. She had been spoilt for a little while. So she figured that, whilst the flat wasn't ideal *now*, it would get better. With time, with some hard work and an awful lot of deep cleaning, she would make it homely. She would paint the walls cream all over and get some fresh flowers to brighten up the rooms. If she got rid of that drab carpet, she could maybe hire a floor buffer and polish the wood underneath.

Naomi knew it could be beautiful. It just needed someone with a good eye for interior design and a bit of imagination. If she applied the same reasoning to her personal life, surely she could make that better, too. All she needed was some time, some space, and then maybe her heart might be ready for love. Naomi at least knew she wanted that now. Despite everything, Tom had still made her realise that she was worth being loved.

Her heart ached as she tried to push away the thought that the person loving her wouldn't be Tom. She had hoped that it would be. But he clearly wasn't ready. Whatever was going on in his head was preventing him from being with her. She had to put Tom and their brief relationship into a closed box. It had been wonderful whilst it had lasted. But she had to accept that their time together in the sun was over now.

At the hospital, Naomi had initially arranged to work opposite shifts to Tom. She had checked his schedule and if he was on days, she would agree to do nights. If he was on lates, she would do the early hours. But still, there were always those moments of handover, the occasional meeting in the locker room where he would look at her with sad eyes and seem to be on the verge of saying something. Except he always remained silent. She wasn't sure what to do. She didn't want to change jobs. She loved working in Welbeck's A&E, especially with all the staff, who had become good friends. But when the matron had mentioned there was an opportunity for one member of the staff to go out on a secondment with the paramedics, Naomi had leapt at the chance.

It was perfect. She'd be out of the department except for the times when they would have to bring in a patient. It would be good for her to get a new perspective on what it was like to be out on the road and on the front line.

She hadn't been in an ambulance since her days of training, when she'd spent a day as an observer. Back then, she'd felt useless and unsure. She'd stood back from the action in her neon-yellow jacket, carrying bags for the paramedics, or fetching and carrying whatever was needed from the truck.

This time, as she clambered on board with the two paramedics, Julia and Luke, she felt sure she would be better.

Stepping outside for a breath of fresh air, Tom saw Naomi clamber on board the ambulance. He paused, unable to tear his eyes away, then he promptly turned around and walked back inside, angry with himself.

His flat was so empty without her! Two weeks she'd been gone and he hadn't realised just how large it was until she'd left and he had been left alone again. He didn't know how he had managed living alone before. Because now when he came home from work, the silence was deafening. The space was endless.

On that first day she'd left, he'd come home from work late, sure that she would be gone, and had wandered into her room. He'd looked about—at the bed where she'd slept, at her empty wardrobe, at her empty drawers. For the time they'd been in his home they'd all been so full of her. The whole flat had been filled with her character, her smile, her laughter. She had managed to imbue the whole place with her spirit and energy and he wasn't sure that he'd ever be able to look at the kitchen again without thinking about her there. His mind had been full of memories of her madly cooking some crazy recipe, whilst singing to the radio, dropping spoons or turning on the blender after forgetting to put on the lid. He'd never forget her burning toast and giving his damn smoke detectors more work than they'd had in years.

He'd moved away from the kitchen and his gaze had fallen on the sofa where they'd made love...

I panicked.

His emotions had been all over the place after they'd made love and the fact that he'd been second-guessing himself hadn't helped matters. He had always been so sure of everything. Had always considered himself to be a clear, logical thinker. After all, with luck on his side, he could save a dying person—he could stem an arterial bleed; he could resuscitate someone. But now, he was flummoxed.

Because he couldn't figure out if he could know whether he was really in love.

It had been so clear-cut with Meredith. There'd been no hesitation there, no doubt. He'd just *known*. But with Naomi…it was like he couldn't think straight with her around. She scrambled his thoughts and toyed with his emotions and he didn't know whether he was coming or going!

Maybe that was love, too.

Maybe it was a different kind of love. Maybe he had been wrong about everything.

He shook his head, trying to clear his thoughts.

He certainly knew how it felt to see Naomi doing everything in her power to not come into contact with him. To see her choosing alternate shifts and volunteering to be with the paramedics. Julia and Luke were great and they'd look after her, he knew that, but…

His chest actually hurt, physically, like his heart was constantly aching with pain. His stomach was all over the place, his concentration was shot.

Perhaps separation was a good thing?

Naomi wandered around her new flat, opening windows, letting in the air before she started yet *another* marathon cleaning session in the flat. Then she turned on the radio, whilst she dusted and scrubbed and cleaned.

It was difficult. Some of the grime was really ingrained and it made her feel sick to look at the state of the dirty water in the bucket she was using. Not that it took much to make her feel sick these days.

She'd noticed it only recently. Her tiredness. Her exhaustion at the end of every day. And then there was the nausea that came whenever she prepared anything to eat. Last night, she'd gone to make herself a tuna sandwich and as soon as she'd opened the tin, the smell had made her heave into the kitchen sink. It was then she'd first wondered if it was something other than pure exhaustion.

She was late, too. She'd never been late. Ever.

She'd bought herself a pregnancy-testing kit, but she hadn't had the courage to use it yet. It had been three weeks since she had slept with Tom, but…

What would she do, if she were pregnant?

If Tom couldn't even love *her*, she didn't know how he would cope with a baby. Would he be able to love it? She hoped so, for the baby's sake. They might not be together as a couple, but she would want him to have a role in their child's life.

But then again, what would that be like for her? She knew immediately that it would be awful. Painful. She couldn't imagine going through a pregnancy, wanting someone to be there to hold her hand through all the scans and tests, not to mention labour and delivery, but knowing the father it wasn't an option.

She was getting carried away. She might not even be pregnant.

But a small part of her willed it to be true. She'd always wanted children, but she'd put that desire on hold during her marriage. Even though she'd known there wasn't a chance of conceiving, every month that had rolled around, bringing with it her next period, had made her feel desperately sad.

She decided she wouldn't take the test until she had cleaned the bathroom. The old avocado suite actually wasn't too bad, but there was mould on the grouting and limescale everywhere. There was no way she would use this bathroom for something so monumental as finding out if she was pregnant, without it being clean to her standards.

She emptied the bucket of water down the sink, swirled

it out with clean and then filled it once again. As she waited for the level to rise she took the pregnancy test out of her handbag and rested it on the sink.

First thing tomorrow you can tell me my future.

She woke suddenly, with trepidation. Amazingly, she'd slept quite well. The exhaustion she'd been feeling had hit her hard last night, after a whole afternoon spent cleaning and scrubbing.

Her stomach roiled as she sat up in bed. Could this be morning sickness? Naomi knew it was possible for a person to believe something with so much conviction that they could convince themselves that they had an illness. It was called psychosomatic disorder. Was it possible that she was wishing so hard that she was pregnant, that she was making herself feel sick?

More importantly, did she really want Tom's baby so badly?

She knew the answer was yes. She did want this baby. And she couldn't think of a better man to be the father. Tom was clever and kind and considerate. He would hopefully be a loving parent, even if he couldn't love Naomi. Even if there could never be any relationship between them as a couple, she couldn't imagine him turning his child away.

She stood up and headed for the bathroom. She knew what she needed to do, but she still read the instructions thoroughly, before following them exactly, and then she laid the test stick on the toilet cistern and waited.

Thirty seconds. She had thirty seconds to wait before she could find out if her life had changed. If it had, she felt sure she could turn it into a positive change. She would make this flat work for her. Make her job work for her, too, until she had to go on maternity leave. With this change, her life could be bright again. Being a single mother was nothing strange these days.

See? I can make myself believe I'll be happy.

Still, a small voice and a large ache in her heart told her that she would never be truly happy without Tom's love. She could tell herself as many times as she liked that this would turn out all right, but until that moment came she knew she would be miserable.

Be realistic, she thought. *Be honest. You want Tom, too.*

Yes, she admitted to herself. She did want him. Even now. Even after all this time that they'd spent apart, she was still haunted by the memory of him, of the way he'd kissed her, made her feel, made her laugh. The way he'd made her feel warm and safe inside.

She loved him. It was an inescapable fact. And whether she was carrying his child or not, she knew she could never have him.

Naomi picked up the test and stared at the result. It was positive. She was pregnant. With Tom's baby.

Never had she ever imagined that she wouldn't be thrilled at discovering she was pregnant. But with the news suddenly in front of her, she only sat there stunned, tears streaming down her face.

She stayed there for ages, just holding the stick in her hands and staring at it. Outside, she could hear the early-morning bustle of traffic—the honking of horns, the sounds of reversing lorries, people calling out in the street. For everyone else, life was carrying on as normal.

But for Naomi, it was as if time had stood still. She kept wondering how she would tell him. What the look on his face would be. He had told her he would never be able to love someone else.

Please, Tom. Be the man that I know that you are and tell me that you'll love our child.

* * *

It was now mid-April and Naomi knew she ought to be over the moon. Deep down inside, somewhere, she felt sure she was rejoicing. It was just that at the moment she felt numb, as if she was still in shock. She would have to tell Tom sooner or later. He had a right to know. Perhaps the best place would be at the Spring Ball in a few days' time? It would be neutral ground and they would be surrounded by people, so his reaction would have to be measured and controlled. They could discuss the issue calmly over a nice glass of champagne.

Oops—no. No alcohol for me.

Fruit juice, then. She picked up the phone and called her local GP surgery. She'd need to see the doctor, and organise getting some folic acid. The doctor would get her registered with a midwife and arrange the first visit once she had got past the first trimester.

She was relieved she hadn't forgotten everything about her maternity training. She could almost pretend that everything was well with the world.

She hoped Tom would take the news calmly and that he would be able to take responsibility and love their child. She didn't like to think about what it might mean if he wasn't able to. Maybe she didn't know him at all.

Surely she hadn't read him wrong. Tom couldn't fail to be a good father, surely. He was charming and dependable and caring. Caring for others was in his DNA. He was a doctor, for crying out loud, and a damned good one on top of that. He loved his work, making sure that others were okay.

An image of him cradling a child in his arms came unbidden to her and she felt an ache deep in the pit of her stomach. She allowed herself to imagine him looking at that child with such intense love.

She imagined him turning to her with the same look in his eyes, and drawing her towards him…

She dashed the image from her mind. She couldn't think of him in that way any more. She couldn't think of him in her arms. Holding her close.

It was all such a mess! She would wait until the evening of the ball and then she would tell him about the baby. She'd agreed to go with Stefan as a friend, not as a date, so she was sure she'd be able to slip away and find Tom.

That was assuming he was *going* to the ball!

CHAPTER TEN

IT WAS THE next weekend and Naomi had arranged to go shopping for her ball gown with Jackie. They went to a variety of stores on the busy London streets, searching for something that appealed. There were rack upon rack of lovely dresses in all colours, shapes and sizes, but still nothing had leapt out at Naomi.

She had been fighting off her exhaustion all morning, sipping from a carton of banana milkshake to stop the pangs of sickness from overwhelming her as they shopped. She didn't want Jackie to suspect she was pregnant, before she'd had a chance to tell Tom. It was only right that he found out first.

Jackie had managed to find her gown in the first store they went into. It was a beautiful off-the-shoulder scarlet dress, quite figure-hugging all the way to her knees, where it suddenly flowed outwards freely. The bodice was highlighted by small diamanté stones and it had looked gorgeous on her as she'd stood on the small podium and twirled in front of the mirror, so that Naomi could see it fully.

'It looks gorgeous on you, Jackie.'

'Oh, thanks. You know people have always said that red is my colour.'

Jackie had stepped down and wriggled back behind the curtain to get changed into her normal clothes.

'They're right. You looked great,' Naomi had added.

Her friend had peered around the curtain at her. 'Pity we can't say the same for you.'

'What?'

'What's going on between you and Tom? One minute you're flatmates, all nice and cosy, and the best of friends, the next you can barely tolerate breathing the same air as him.'

Naomi had briefly seen a vision of herself in Tom's arms, feeling cherished and adored and *loved*. Then she'd pushed the image away. He hadn't thought about it the same way. 'We had a difference in opinion.'

'What about?'

'I'd rather not talk about it. I've moved on.'

'You've moved flat! Stefan tells me you're in his block now. How's that working out for you?'

It's horrible, she'd thought. *I hate that flat. It's not home. It's not me!*

'Yeah, it's good.'

'It sounds like a lot of work from what Stefan tells me. You need a hand?'

'Er…maybe. Yeah. We could have one of those wallpaper-stripping parties.'

Jackie had swished the curtain open, dressed in her normal clothes once again. 'Please tell me you don't have a woodchip nightmare?'

Naomi had nodded and laughed when she'd seen the look of horror on her friend's face. 'I do.'

'Oh, shoot. That's such a delight to remove!'

Jackie had paid for her dress and, once it had been wrapped in tissue paper, boxed and bagged, they'd headed out of the shop.

Now they were trying yet another store, still searching for something for Naomi.

'How's A&E?' she asked as they wandered. 'What am I missing?'

'Not much. You should know—you bring in half the cases! How are you enjoying your time with the paramedics?'

'It's good. Interesting, but…'

'It's not A&E.'

'No.'

'Do you miss it?'

She nodded.

'You miss Tom, too, don't you?'

Naomi tried not to make eye contact with her friend, but Jackie was persistent. She stepped in front of her, forcing her to look at her. 'Naomi!'

'Yes! Yes, I do.'

'Even though you were *only* flatmates?'

She coloured.

'I *knew* it! I knew there was more to it than what you were letting on! What happened?'

'I don't really want to talk about it. It upsets me. Please, Jackie. Don't say anything to anyone. Least of all Stefan. He's such a gossip.'

Jackie threaded her arm through Naomi's. 'My lips are sealed. But, you know, I will say one thing.'

'What?'

'That that man cares for you beyond belief. He's miserable now; he's like a robot again. He's acting just the way he did after his wife died. I don't know what he's done to upset you, Naomi, but he loves you. You mark my words.'

She stared straight ahead.

No, he doesn't.

It didn't matter what Jackie said. Tom didn't love her.

He'd told her he was incapable of it. He'd said he didn't believe in a second chance at love.

You mark my words...he loves you...

She smiled sadly. If only that were true. It was nice of Jackie to say that, but Naomi didn't need to hear it. It only gave her false hope. But she wouldn't be able to cope if she went to him and told him that she loved *him* and he threw it back in her face. If it were true, and Jackie were right, then it needed to come from Tom. And Naomi already knew that would never happen.

Jackie said no more about Tom as they continued to shop. And eventually, Naomi found a wonderful dress in midnight blue. It was ankle-length, one-shouldered, and it had a beautiful black lace overlay around the waist. They found a gorgeous red clutch to contrast with it, which wasn't hugely expensive. Naomi decided this would be her last extravagance. All her future funds would have to go towards the flat and things for the baby. But this dress would be her swansong to being a single woman. After this, if all went well, she would be a single *mother*. She briefly wondered what Vincent would have said, if he could have seen her. She hoped that he would have been proud.

She was suddenly glad she was going to the ball. It was a fitting way to end this current chapter in her life.

'I've probably made a mistake in accepting Stefan's invite,' she confessed to Jackie.

'Stefan is full of himself. But he's a decent guy underneath all that rubbish he doles out.'

Naomi twirled in front of the mirror in her dress, eyeing the gown and trying to see if her pregnancy showed, which of course it didn't—it was still early days. Thank goodness. No one would guess her secret. No one would tell Tom until she'd had the chance to see him first.

CHAPTER ELEVEN

TOM WAS HARD at work in A&E. Unable to cope with the maelstrom of thoughts in his head about Naomi, he'd sought solace the way he had used to do, treating the sick and injured.

So far that day he'd seen a cardiac arrest, a tree surgeon who had fallen over twenty feet onto his back, some victims from a bad road-traffic accident and a query stroke victim.

Work had been the only way he'd been able to make himself feel better after Meredith's death. And so he'd expected his work to have the same effect after everything that had happened with Naomi.

But it wasn't working. His head was still in a spin. He wasn't his normal calm, polite self. Instead, he was being terse. Curt. His temper felt extremely short and every time he caught himself snapping at someone, he would inwardly berate himself.

All he could think about was Naomi.

His neat, stable little world had crumpled in on itself. He could barely keep himself upright. He could barely keep putting one foot in front of the other, without thinking about her, wishing that he'd acted differently, wishing it all could have *ended* differently.

He'd sworn to himself after Meredith had died that he'd

never again go through that pain of losing someone that he loved. He'd promised never to expose himself to that all-consuming grief that he'd experienced once before.

But wasn't he suffering now anyway? He was certainly already in pain. And was that because he loved Naomi? Was he feeling this pain and uncertainty, all because he was denying himself the woman that he loved?

His brow rumpled in thought. If he admitted to himself that perhaps he did love Naomi, *then* what would happen? He didn't know if there was any point in telling her. He'd already messed her around once, upset her, so he doubted she'd want to listen to him now. It was too late. He'd already told her he couldn't love another.

He winced as he recalled his words.

If Naomi had any sense, she would run a mile. He'd used her. Unwittingly maybe. Naively, perhaps. But still, she'd said he had opened her eyes to possibilities in her life. That he'd made her realise a need for love that she'd closed the door on, just as he had. She'd just opened that door earlier than he had. She'd been ready to cope with it, ready to risk love again.

The question was…was he ready?

He was suffering so much now, because there was so much distance between them, when what he really wanted was the opposite. He'd imposed a self-built barrier of fear. And just as he'd done that, she too had tried to protect herself by moving away from him.

They'd both thought they had been protecting themselves, but in reality they hadn't. They'd only caused themselves more hurt, because they'd believed that the alternative could only lead to pain.

But what if I allowed myself to love again? What if Naomi gave me another chance and said yes?
Tom looked down at his paperwork. There was still so

much he needed to do. Yet the Spring Ball was just a few hours away and Naomi was going with Stefan. He was a decent nurse, but still... *Stefan*? The hospital Lothario? Tom couldn't bear the idea.

He glanced at the clock, trying to make his decision.

Suddenly he knew exactly where he had to go.

Tom knelt in front of the headstone and laid the bunch of calla lilies on Meredith's grave. Then he stood back and looked hard at the words and letters etched into the stone.

Meredith Williams
Beloved Wife

He cleared his throat.

'Meredith? I need to tell you...that I love you. That I will *always* love you and there will always be a treasured space for you in my heart, but...I've met someone. Her name's Naomi.'

His gaze drifted from his wife's name to her photograph embedded in the stone within a golden heart. He looked at that smiling face, the twinkle in her eyes, remembering her as she'd beamed at the camera on that day so long ago.

'You'd like her. She's a nurse, like you. Spirited. Funny. Passionate. Caring.' He sighed and his shoulders dropped as he looked up and past the other stones, across the empty field to the trees in the distance, gathering his thoughts. Gathering more words.

'She means an awful lot to me and that surprised me because I didn't think anyone could mean anything to me any more.' He reached out to touch the cold stone. 'I want to be with her. She may not want me, after the way I've treated her, but at least I'm thinking clearly now. I know what I want and I *know* that you, more than anyone else in the world, would want me to be happy. So I'm going to try.'

He stood there for a few more quiet moments, listening to the birds singing in the nearby trees, and spotted a squirrel scratching at the ground a few metres away. Even a rabbit had dared to venture out from the hedgerow, but it scurried away as soon as it noticed him.

Tom turned back to his wife's picture and sucked in a deep breath. This was it. His decision. He was moving forward now. He couldn't live his life the way he had for eight years. He'd been in limbo and it was all so clear to him now. Before Naomi had come into his life, and he'd just thought of himself as a widower, he had convinced himself that was it. That that was the way his life was going to be for the rest of his days. But he'd been wrong. He'd been so utterly wrong.

His feelings for Naomi had been so unexpected, so sudden. He had been like a man on death row who had been told that in actual fact he was being set free.

Naomi had set him free and he was no longer a prisoner. He'd done his time.

Tom gazed at Meredith's picture. He didn't feel sadness. He didn't feel regret.

He felt content. Right.

He felt *sure*.

'Goodbye, Meredith.' He touched his fingers to the stone one final time and closed his eyes, feeling the soft breeze on his face, and it was as if he knew she was telling him it was okay. A smile reached his face.

Opening his eyes, he began to walk away.

He didn't need to look back.

Naomi was getting ready for the ball. There was none of the excitement that she once would have had at the thought of such an event. Her dress was beautiful and Jackie had taken up her hair for her, which was now held in place by bejewelled pins. Looking in the mirror, as she finished her make-up, she felt she truly did look like the princess that Jackie had told her she would be.

But she didn't feel like one. She didn't feel the happiness she knew she ought to be feeling. After all, this was going to be her big goodbye, her first and last large event with the department. She'd decided that, after this, she would work out the months she had before she gave birth but then she would leave Welbeck. She would be the best mother to her child that she could be. She'd been given this opportunity, after all this time, and she was going to embrace it.

As she slipped on her heels and put on her bracelet and matching earrings, she tried to find the smile that had been missing from her face for so long.

She popped a small piece of ginger into her mouth. She'd been chewing on small pieces for a few days now. It seemed to help that awful sick feeling in her stomach that seemed to be there on a permanent basis. She took a deep breath.

When they arrived, she would plaster on that fake smile, be gracious and pleasant. She would greet people, all the while hating every minute, scanning the room, knowing that she had to talk to Tom.

Stefan arrived in his tuxedo, and she had to admit he looked rather charming, but she only felt sadness when she met him at the door. She felt it should have been Tom standing there.

There was a slight evening breeze, and the cool air danced around her bare arms and back as they went outside and climbed into the taxi. Stefan chatted amiably as they travelled and she tried to seem attentive. When they finally arrived at the hotel, she slowly made her way up the steps into the building and then suddenly, with her nerves racing, they entered the ballroom.

It was magnificent. It was as if they'd stepped inside a palace. Jackie had been right: the events team had really pulled out all the stops to make the place look magical. There were high vaulted ceilings lit by chandeliers and fluted lights lined the walls. Past all the porticoes and columns, Naomi could see a small orchestra in the corner, and could hear someone very talented playing the grand piano at its centre. Everyone was dressed in their finery—the men in tuxedoes and the women in beautiful ball gowns of every conceivable colour. Waiters covered the room like silent hummingbirds, offering drinks and canapés on silver trays as people clinked champagne glasses, laughing and chattering.

If only everything were different.

She wanted to be able to enjoy it. She could certainly appreciate all the hard work that had gone into the occasion. The fact that she couldn't be here with the one person she wanted the most made her sad, tearful almost.

There were already a few couples dancing in the centre of the floor. She would have loved to dance with Tom and be close to him again, the way they had been at the roller disco. The image came to her of being in his arms, laughing, pressed up close against his chest. She could almost feel his heart pounding away, her hands in his as they had stared deeply into each other's eyes…

She wiped away a small tear and offered Stefan a brave smile. 'It's gorgeous!' she exclaimed as she followed her date down the steps into the room.

It was warm and so many people were wearing perfumes or aftershave that the aroma started to make her feel queasy. Laying a hand upon her stomach, she took a glass from a passing waiter's tray and sipped at it to help wet her dry mouth.

Ugh. Alcohol.

She looked around for another drink, searching for something that looked like fruit juice, but as she turned away she lost sight of Stefan. Suddenly she was left in the middle of the ballroom all alone.

So this is what it feels like to be lonely in a crowd, she thought.

Jostled and bustled, she tried to make her way over to one side of the room where she could hide. There was a line of tables with a buffet selection. She wondered if she might find something there to help settle her stomach.

A few people she knew recognised her, greeting her with air kisses. Then she moved on again, telling herself that if she couldn't find Tom, she would only stay for an hour. She would make sure she'd said hello to everyone she knew, then she would make her excuses and go.

She felt a hand on her arm and she turned, expecting to find Stefan standing there.

Tom!

All of a sudden her stomach began churning wildly, her mouth grew dry and she almost couldn't speak. She couldn't believe how good it was to see him here! He looked absolutely dashing in his perfect tuxedo, staring at her, as if…as if he couldn't bear to look anywhere else.

'Tom?'

He was *here*. Which meant that she would be able to tell him about the baby. She'd been worried that he wouldn't turn up, and that she would have to find him at work. But now, the moment was here. She would have to stand in front of him and tell him that his world was about to change! That he was going to become a father. She would tell him that she would stay out of his way if that was what he wanted—even if it would kill her to do so—but she prayed that he would love and cherish their baby.

He would make a good dad, she felt sure of that. Perhaps he might be the one to teach their child to ride a bike? He would be patient, she knew; supportive, encouraging.

Tears were welling in her eyes again.

She blinked furiously, and dabbed at the corners of her eyes, hoping the tears wouldn't fall and betray her.

Tom gave her a small smile.

'Naomi. May I speak with you? Privately?' He seemed serious and Naomi wondered what this could be about. She wondered if he was going to discuss work with her. Maybe he wanted to talk about what would happen now that her secondment with the paramedics was coming to an end.

She didn't see the need for privacy if that was the case, but she was keen to get out of the crowd. She wanted to get away from the mixture of scents and the cacophony of too many people in one room.

'Sure,' she said.

'There's a small foyer over there.' Tom pointed and then took her arm as he escorted her through the crowds.

She tried not to think too hard about his arm tucked through hers. It was a too painful reminder of everything that she couldn't have. She wished he wouldn't touch her at all. That would be easier.

When they got to the foyer, he let go of her arm and closed the doors behind them, shutting out the noise of the chatter and the soft piano music. She breathed in deeply, relishing the fresher air coming in through the open windows.

Now that they were here, he stood in front of her, looking a little unsure of how to start.

'What's wrong?'

He licked his lips and stared at her for a moment. Then he spoke.

'Naomi? First off, I just want to say that I'm sorry. *Dreadfully* sorry for the way I reacted to you that night we were together.' He reached for her hands and held them in his as he faced her. 'That night was the most amazing thing in the world to me because it opened my eyes. No...not just my eyes. But my heart...my soul. I'd kept them locked away, determined that no one would ever have the chance to tear me apart again, but being with you...being with you made me realise that I *could* love again. That I could take that chance and risk my heart because I loved you.

'It scared me. It sent me into a whirlwind of confusion and shock. I hadn't known it was possible to care for someone that much for a second time and when you told me that I'd shown you that love was possible, I'll admit I was frightened. It was all too clear that you'd changed me in the same way and I wasn't ready to accept that it was okay. But I am ready now.'

She stared up at him, tears now openly falling down her cheeks as his words pierced her heart and the barriers she'd been putting up to protect herself. Those barriers were crumbling away, breaking into a million tiny pieces at every word he said.

'I know I hurt you—I'm sorry. I know I shut you out—I'm sorry. I can't say it enough to make amends for all the pain I caused you and I know that I have no right to expect you to forgive me. But I'm asking you to consider it. I'm asking you to find forgiveness in your heart; if not now, then maybe some time in the future, I don't know. I just need to tell you that I love you. And if you'll have me, then I'll be here for you until the end of time.'

Naomi sobbed, wanting to wipe the tears away, but at the same time unwilling to let go of his hands.

He *loved* her?

She laughed through her tears, knowing she must look a mess, but too happy to care.

'Oh, Tom! I do forgive you. I do. I'm sorry I put you through so much torment. And that I caused you this much pain in the first place! There you'd been, working your way through life, knowing exactly what you wanted from it, and I came along and turned it upside down.'

'I needed you to turn it upside down.'

'I needed *you*. You showed me what real love could be. It wasn't just the physical stuff, but also the incredible companionship, the time we spent together, having fun, taking risks—'

'The burnt dinners?'

She laughed. 'Yes! The burnt dinners…I told you what that all meant to me before you were ready to hear it. I knew what you'd been through, that you were uncertain, and yet I couldn't hold it back because I was so determined to be open and honest about how I felt. Because you know something? Even though I loved Vincent, I wasn't open and honest with him. I always kept my feelings about everything locked inside, because I didn't want to upset him, or worry him, because I thought he already had so much to deal with. But with you…' she squeezed his fingers in hers '…I was overwhelmed by my feelings. I spoke without thinking, but…I love you, too, Tom. You know that I do. It's torn my heart to pieces spending this time apart.'

'Me too.'

'I love you. I want to be with you.'

'I love you, Naomi.'

He dipped his head to kiss her, but she backed away and he looked at her, confused.

'What?'

'There's something else.'

'Oh?'

'*Someone* else.'

His eyes darkened and he glanced at the double doors leading to the ballroom. 'Stefan?'

She shook her head. 'No.'

Tom looked puzzled. 'Then who?' he asked, appearing to brace himself.

She smiled and blushed. 'I can't believe I get to tell you this and actually be happy about it.'

He stared at her, waiting for the axe to fall.

'I'm pregnant, Tom. With our baby.'

His mouth dropped open, then he gulped and glanced down at her abdomen, a smile slowly appearing on his face. 'You're pregnant?'

She nodded.

'Oh, Naomi!' He pulled her to him and kissed her.

Naomi was so filled with happiness to be in his arms again that she thought she might burst! She'd never expected this when she'd set out that evening, not even knowing whether Tom would be there. She'd pictured herself telling him about the baby, expecting it to be sombre and sad, with him dutifully promising to be involved. Her heart had almost broken there and then, imagining the scenario.

But here she was. Tom loved her. He wanted to be with her and he was thrilled about the baby!

They would raise their child *together*. As a *couple*. Not as single parents, as she'd been prepared to do.

His lips against hers were like magic. She tingled in every place that they touched. Her heart was singing. The dark clouds that had hovered over her earlier had dissipated and she felt like they were both standing in bright sunshine. They were together and strong. And together they would be able to tackle anything. Apart, they'd been broken and weak.

Not any longer.

Now the future looked bright. Optimistic. Full of promise and expectation.

Tom broke the kiss and smiled down at her, then he reached into his pocket and dropped to one knee.

Naomi gasped.

'Naomi Bloom. You fell into my arms the first day that we met and I want you to stay there until the day that we die. I love you more than life and you would make me the happiest man alive if you would do me the honour of marrying me.'

He opened the small box he was holding and she saw a beautiful diamond solitaire nestled in its bed of navy velvet.

'I will!'

Tom beamed as he took the ring from the box and gently slipped it onto her finger. Then he pulled her to him once again and kissed her.

Her body sang for him. Her heart soared.

This was the love she'd known was possible. *This* was what she'd dreamed about when she'd set off to London to find her own way in the world. Here was her chance to find love again. And the fact that it was with Tom, the most wonderful man she had ever known, made it more than perfect.

She couldn't be happier. It just wasn't possible.

The noise from beyond the double doors rose an octave, reminding them that the real world still awaited them. Including Naomi's date for the evening.

'What about Stefan?' she asked, smiling.

'He can be an usher.'

'I came here with him. I owe him an explanation.'

Tom held out his arm for her. 'Then we'll tell him together. I don't think even Stefan will stand in the way of true love.'

Naomi laid her head against his shoulder. 'We almost did,' she said, sucking in a breath as she realised what they'd almost lost.

'We found our way in the end.'

She looked up at him. 'I could never lose you again.'

He kissed her. 'You won't have to. We have eternity together.'

They both took in a deep breath and then they pushed open the double doors.

EPILOGUE

HE COULDN'T QUITE believe it. It was almost time. All these months of waiting. Of watching Naomi's tummy grow, of feeling those magical kicks through her skin and marvelling at the life beneath, wondering just *who* was in there.

Tom hadn't known he could be this happy. To think of where he had been even a year ago, believing there was nothing left in his life to be glad about…and yet here he was, about to become a father.

Imminently.

'Come on, Naomi…*push*!' He gripped her hand, holding it against his chest, glancing from her scrunched-up face to the midwife and then down to see if he could see their baby's head yet.

'Baby's coming, Naomi. One huge push for me now!' urged the midwife.

Naomi sucked in a deep breath and focused. She gave this push her all, every tiny bit of strength that she had left. Fourteen hours of labour were nearly at an end. She was sweating. Her hair was plastered to her face.

Tom felt her squeeze his fingers as she groaned and grimaced, before she let out her breath and then immediately sucked in another, ready to push again. The midwife stopped her.

'Here's the head! Just pant for me now…pant, pant, that's it. And just a tiny push for me.'

Tom looked down. They were nearly there. His baby's head and face were emerging. 'Look at all that hair!'

Naomi looked up at him and began to cry. 'Really?'

'Really.' He kissed her forehead. 'You're doing it! You're doing it! I love you so much!'

'Get ready, Dad. Are you going to cut the cord?'

Tom nodded, beaming at the midwife. 'Try and stop me.' He watched anxiously as the baby turned naturally and the midwife checked for a cord around the neck, but everything was fine.

'One last push and you'll have your baby in your arms.'

Naomi nodded and smiled, before giving one last almighty push, the effort of which caused her to cry out.

Their baby was finally fully born, crying, into the world and the midwife lifted the squirming bundle straight onto Naomi's stomach.

Tom wasn't sure when he had started crying. Had it been the moment he saw his beautiful baby? Or maybe when he'd seen Naomi's face, so full of love, as she cradled their child?

'Here you go, Daddy. Cut between these two clips.' The midwife handed him the scissors and Tom cut the cord in disbelief, tears streaming down his cheeks. 'Do you want to see what you have?' she asked.

Tom was almost afraid to touch the baby. It was so beautiful, so precious! But he rolled it gently onto its back to reveal the sex. 'We have a daughter!'

Naomi held her tightly, lifting up her top so that their daughter could nestle against her skin. 'A baby girl!'

The midwife smiled broadly. 'Do we have a name?'

Naomi looked up at Tom and smiled. 'We do.'

He laid his hand on his daughter's tiny head as he announced her name. 'Sophia Grace.'

He gazed down at his beautiful fiancée and his darling daughter, unable to believe that they were both his. That they were here with him. Safe. Together. Loved. He bent to gently kiss his daughter's cheek and marvelled how soft her skin was. 'I love you both so much,' he murmured softly. He looked up at Naomi and they kissed, their tears of happiness mingling, their joy immeasurable.

'I love you, too. I'm the luckiest woman in the world.'

He kissed her again, still in disbelief at what he'd just witnessed. He had a child! A beautiful, perfect baby girl, who he already loved so much and wanted to protect until the end of the earth. With love overflowing from his heart, he closed his eyes and kissed his daughter's head as he cradled both of them in his arms, unable to believe that all of this happiness, all of this joy, was his.

'Thank you,' he said, when the afterbirth had been delivered and the midwife had left them alone. 'For coming into my life. For falling into my arms and refusing to give up on me.'

She touched her forehead to his and smiled, tears of elation still on her cheeks. 'You're worth it.'

'Having so much…all this happiness, all this love…'

She laid her hand upon his cheek and brought his lips down to hers. 'We don't need to be afraid of it.'

'I know. I'll cherish every second I spend with you and Sophia.'

'And I'll cherish them, too.'

The midwife returned to take the baby to clean her up and check her APGAR score, then she handed Sophia back, placing her carefully into Tom's arms.

Sophia, swaddled and warm, blinked at the harsh lights in the room, then gazed up into her father's face.

Tom stroked his daughter's cheek, full of pride and love. Then he looked to the woman he loved just as much and reached out to hold her hand.

Together they were strong.

Together they could face anything.

* * * * *

MILLS & BOON®

MEDICAL ROMANCE™

THE ULTIMATE IN ROMANTIC MEDICAL DRAMA

A sneak peek at next month's titles...

In stores from 24th March 2016:

- **Seduced by the Heart Surgeon** – Carol Marinelli *and* **Falling for the Single Dad** – Emily Forbes

- **The Fling That Changed Everything** – Alison Roberts *and* **A Child to Open Their Hearts** – Marion Lennox

- **The Greek Doctor's Secret Son** – Jennifer Taylor

- **Caught in a Storm of Passion** – Lucy Ryder

Available at WHSmith, Tesco, Asda, Eason, Amazon and Apple

Just can't wait?
Buy our books online a month before they hit the shops!
visit www.millsandboon.co.uk

These books are also available in eBook format!

MILLS & BOON®

Helen Bianchin v Regency Collection!

0316_MB520

MILLS & BOON®

Why shop at millsandboon.co.uk?

Each year, thousands of romance readers find their perfect read at millsandboon.co.uk. That's because we're passionate about bringing you the very best romantic fiction. Here are some of the advantages of shopping at www.millsandboon.co.uk:

* **Get new books first**—you'll be able to buy your favourite books one month before they hit the shops

* **Get exclusive discounts**—you'll also be able to buy our specially created monthly collections, with up to 50% off the RRP

* **Find your favourite authors**—latest news, interviews and new releases for all your favourite authors and series on our website, plus ideas for what to try next

* **Join in**—once you've bought your favourite books, don't forget to register with us to rate, review and join in the discussions

Visit **www.millsandboon.co.uk**
for all this and more today!